THE WIG

CHARLES WRIGHT
THE WIG

WITH AN INTRODUCTION BY **ISHMAEL REED**

NEA HERITAGE & PRESERVATION SERIES

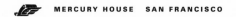 MERCURY HOUSE   SAN FRANCISCO

Published in the United States by Mercury House, San Francisco, California, a nonprofit publishing company devoted to the free exchange of ideas and guided by a dedication to literary values. Mercury House and colophon are registered trademarks of Mercury House, Incorporated. Visit us at www.mercuryhouse.org.

United States Constitution, First Amendment: Congress shall make no law respecting an establishment of religion, or prohibiting the free exercise thereof; or abridging the freedom of speech, or of the press; or the right of the people peaceably to assemble, and to petition the Government for a redress of grievances.

Author photo and cover art, "Escape," by Phelonise Willie.

Cover design by Scott di Girolamo. Interior design by K. Janene-Nelson. Editorial and production work by Heather Ambler, Nicholas Buzanski, Justin Edgar, and Jeremy Lindston. Special thanks go to the National Endowment for the Arts and to author David Meltzer, for inspiration.

Printed on acid-free paper and manufactured by McNaughton & Gunn, MI.

Library of Congress Cataloging in Publication Data:

Wright, Charles, 1932–
    The wig / Charles Wright ; with an introduction by Ishmael Reed.
      p. cm. — (NEA Heritage & Preservation series ; 2)
    ISBN 1-56279-127-3 (acid-free paper)
    1. Harlem (New York, N.Y.)—Fiction. 2. African American men—Fiction.
    3. Young men—Fiction. I. Title. II. Series.
    PS3573.R532W75 2003
    813'.6—dc21
                            2002155520

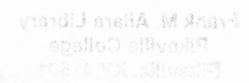

FOR
CHARLES TRABUE ROBB

AND IN MEMORY OF
LOWNEY TURNER HANDY

INTRODUCTION

I was living in the Chelsea district of New York when I read Charles Wright's *The Wig*. As someone who was looking for something fresh, something that broke the model of the monotonous predictable conventional novel, I found it to be an exciting read. My friend Steve Cannon, who was later to write the *Wig*-influenced *Groove Bang and Jive Around*, read it too. Steve and I located Charles Wright and visited him at the Albert Hotel, a hotel made famous by Chester Himes having resided there at one time. Wright's style reminded me of Himes. Comic in a sardonic manner, absurd, surrealist, campy, hip, Jazzy, all of the elements that interested me. This was a leap-about, stream-of-the-unconscious book. Accustomed to the discontinuity of television, where the narrative is constantly interrupted, I wasn't confused at all by Wright's manner of writing. But it seems the critics of the day were confused, and many chose to overlook *The Wig*'s unique merits.

From the first allusion-busy paragraph until the book's conclusion, the reader is taken on a roller coaster, fun house excursion. This is a true Be-Bop novel that jumps about like Bird's solo "Blues For Alice," a tune that adds new chords to the old twelve-bar blues. Parker changes. Wright changes. In one paragraph alone we have Mongolia, Arabs, Greenwich Village, Andre Gide, an African coffeehouse, Ivy League derelicts, Napoleon fever, and a Zen Buddhist. Very few American writers have Charles Wright's range; on the literary landscape of the 1960s, Wright's *The Wig* was a red-winged black bird amidst a crowd of pigeons.

The characters are memorable and eccentric. Mr. Fishback, the necrophilic funeral director; the interminably pregnant Nonnie Swift; the transvestite Miss Sandra Hanover; Little Jimmie, the former movie star; and Madam X, who provides a permanent cure for love. The gallows humor is hilarious, but the humor is deadly as Wright targets individuals and institutions. Blumstein's Department store sells human-hair rugs, "clipped from live Negro traitors." Shoe shiners invent a "dust machine": "The dust shoeshine boy stands on the corner with the machine in a shopping bag from Macy's, rolling his white eyeballs and sucking a slice of candied watermelon. You know. Like he's waiting on his mama. Every time a likely customer walks by, the dust shiner pulls the magic string. By the time the customer reaches the middle of the block he sure need a shine." A scene in the Black Disaster Diner permits the author to comment on police corruption. Hollywood and Consumerism are subjected to some barbs. And even though these satirical hits are done in his self-deprecating manner, one still feels the sting. Charles Wright is a literary possum-player.

The lead character, Lester Jefferson, and his various occupations are symbolic of the humiliation that black men must endure, daily. For $90 for five and a half days, plus all the chicken he could eat on his day off, he goes through the streets, on his hands and knees, crying "Cock-a-doodle-doo. Cock-a-doodle-do. Eat me. Eat Me. All over town. Eat me at the King of Southern-Fried Chicken." In another scene he picks up change by tap dancing in front of the Empire State Building. Throughout, he romps through these bizarre situations wearing a "magnificent burnished red-golden halo."

Charles Wright's novel marked a change in African-American fiction; it had neither the lofty and Biblical heft of James Baldwin's works, nor the opaque elusiveness and obeisance to New York Intellectual fashion found in Ellison's *Invisible Man*. It was Richard Pryor before there was a Richard Pryor. Richard Pryor on paper. All of us who wanted to "experiment," as we were seeing our painter and musician friends experiment, used it as a model. And though some would call me the literary son of Ralph Ellison, in the 1960s I was the younger brother of Charles Wright. The fact that this novel was ignored tells a lot about how African-American fiction has been kept in its place. But a classic refuses to remain in its place.

Ishmael Reed
Oct. 21, 2002

THE WIG

AUTHOR'S NOTE

THE WORD **WIG** AS IT IS USED IN THIS STORY IS NEGRO
SLANG FOR **HAIR**

AND THE STORY ITSELF IS SET IN AN AMERICA OF
TOMORROW

1

"EVERY PHENOMENON HAS ITS NATURAL CAUSE ..."

—JAMES JOYCE

ONE

I was a desperate man. Quarterly, I got that crawly feeling in my wafer-thin stomach. During these fasting days, I had the temper of a Greek mountain dog. It was hard to maintain a smile; everyone seemed to jet toward the goal of The Great Society, while I remained in the outhouse, penniless, without "connections." Pretty girls, credit cards, charge account, Hart Schaffner & Marx suits, fine shoes, Dobbs hats, XK-E Jaguars, and more pretty girls cluttered my butterscotch-colored dreams. Lord—I'd work like a slave, but how to acquire an acquisitional gimmick? Mercy—something had to fall from the tree of fortune! Tom-toms were signaling to my frustrated brain; the message: I had to make it.

As a consequence, I was seized with a near epileptic fit early one Thursday morning. I stood in the center of my shabby though genteel furnished room, shivering and applauding vigorously. Sweet Jesus!—my King James-shaped head vaulted toward the fungus-covered ceiling pipes where cockroach acrobatics had already begun. The cockroaches seemed extraordinarily lively, as if they too were taking part in the earth-shaking revelation. Even the late March sun was soft and sweet as moonlight, and the beautiful streets of Harlem were strangely quiet.

Smiling ecstatically, tears gushing from my Dutch-almond eyes, I recalled what the man in the drugstore had said: "With this, you may become whatever you desire."

Indeed, I *did* have a Mongolian chance, perhaps even a brilliant future; the black clouds would soon recede. I had tried so hard. Masqueraded as a silent Arab waiter in an authentic North African coffeehouse in Greenwich Village. I'd been quite successful too. Tempting dreamers of Gide, Ivy League derelicts, and hungry pseudo-virgins. Barefoot, marijuana-eyed, fezzed, wearing nothing under my candy-stripe djellaba, I was finally unmasked by two old-maid sisters, one club-footed, both with mushroom-colored mustaches, who had lived for a decade in Morocco. The sisters swooned at the deception, left a two-dollar tip and their hashish-scented calling card. Those sisters turned me on, and that night I had a mild attack of Napoleon fever and began insulting the customers. The Zen Buddhist owner was going to New Zealand anyway.

What happened after that? More of the crawly worms in the stomach. Misery. I tap-danced in front of the Empire State Building for a week and collected only one dollar and twenty-seven cents. I was refused unemployment insurance, maybe because I looked foreign and spoke almost perfect English. Naturally, I could have got on welfare, but who has the guts to stand on the stoop, hands in pockets, chewing on a toothpick ten hours a day, watching little kids pass by, their big eyes staring up at you like the eyes of extras in some war movie? There are some things a man can't do.

No, a man tries another gimmick. But what? For me a Spanish façade would be simple, but very uncool. Filipino? American Indian? I wondered. Eurasian might provide a fetish glamour. Was I capable of bringing off a Jewish exterior? I wondered. Becoming a nice little white Protestant was clearly impossible. Born with a vermeil question mark in my mouth, twenty-one years ago, I have been called the son of the Devil; my social security card is silent on the point of whether or not I'm human. I suppose that's why I'm slightly schizophrenic.

Hump psyche reports! I was going to attack *my* future.

I rushed to the bathroom, the meeting place of exactly seventy-five Negroes of various racial origins. Standing rigidly, religiously, in the white-tiled room, my heart exploded in my eyes like the sea. My brain whirled.

Do not the auburn-haired gain a new sense of freedom as a blonde (see *Miss Clairol*)? Who can deny the madness of a redesigned nose (see *Miami Beach*)? The first conference of Juvenile Delinquents met in Riis Park and there was absolutely no violence: a resolution was passed to send Seconal, zip guns, airplane glue, and contraceptives to the Red Chinese (see *The Daily News*). The American Medical Association announced indignantly that U.S. abortion and syphilis quotas are far below the world average (see Channel 2). Modern gas stations have coin-operated air pumps in the ladies' room so the under-blessed may inflate their skimpy boobs (see *Dorothy Kil-gallen*). Undercover homosexuals sneak into the local drug-stores and receive plastic though workable instruments plus bonus Daisy trade stamps (see *Compliments of a new-found friend*). Schizo wisdom? Remember, I said to myself, you are living in the greatest age mankind has known. Whereupon, I went to the washbasin, picked up the Giant Economy jar of long-lasting Silky Smooth Hair Relaxer, with the Built-in Sweat-proof Base (*trademark registered*). Carefully, I read the directions. The red, white, and gold label guarantees that the user can go deep-sea diving, emerge from the water, and shake his head triumphantly like any white boy. This miracle with the scent of wild roses looks like vanilla ice cream and is capable of soften-ing in sufficiently Negroid hands.

I took a handful of Silky Smooth and began massaging my scalp. Then, just to be on the safe side, I added Pre-cautionary Oil, thick, odorless, indigenous to the Georgia swamps. Massaging deftly, I remembered that old-fash-ioned hair aids were mixed with yak dung and lye. They burned the scalp and if the stuff got in your eye you could go blind from it. One thing was certain: you combed out scabs of dried blood for a month. But a compassionate Northern Senator had the hair aids outlawed. Said he, in ringing historic words: "Mr. Chairman, I offer an amend-ment to this great Spade tragedy! These people are real Americans and we should outlaw all hair aids that makes them lose their vibrations and éclat." Silky Smooth (using a formula perfected by a Lapp tribe in Karasiok, Norway) posed no problems.

Yes indeed. A wild excitement engulfed me. My mirrored image reflected, in an occult fashion, a magnificent future. I hadn't felt so good since discovering last year that I actually disliked watermelon.

But the next step was the most difficult act of my life. I had to wait five minutes until the pomade penetrated, stiffened, evaporated. Five minutes of suffering. I stood tall like the great-great-grandson of slaves, sharecroppers, Old World royalty. Tall, like a storm trooper, like an Honor Scout. Yes! I'd stalk that druggist if the experiment failed. Lord—it couldn't fail! I'm Walter Mitty's target-colored stepson. Sweet dreams zipped through my mind. A politician had prophesied that it was extremely likely a Negro would be elected President of the United States in the year 2000. Being realistic, I could just picture myself as Chairman of the Handyman's Union, addressing the Committee on Foreign Relations and then being castrated. At least I'd no longer have to phone Mr. Fishback, the necrophilic funeral director, each time I went downtown. What a relief that would be. The dimes I'd save!

While the stuff dried I thought of Mr. Fishback. Sweet Daddy Fish, Nonnie called him, but Nonnie liked to put the bad mouth on people. I owed Mr. Fishback for my latest (was it counterfeit?) credit card.

Beams of the morning sun danced through the ice-cube-sized window as I began to wash the pomade out of my hair. I groaned powerfully. The texture of my hair *had* changed. Before reaching for a towel, I couldn't resist looking in the cracked mirror while milky-colored water ran down my flushed face.

Hail Caesar and all dead Cotton Queens! Who the hell ever said only a rake could get through those gossamer locks?

Indeed! I prayed. I laughed. I shook my head and watched each silky curl fall into place. I had only one regret: I wished there were a little wind blowing, one just strong enough to give me a wind-swept look; then I'd be able to toss a nonchalant lock from my forehead. I'd been practicing for a week and had the bit down solid.

You could borrow an electric fan, I was telling myself, and just then I heard Nonnie Swift scream.

"Help! Won't somebody please help me?" The voice came from the hall.

Let the brandy bitch scream her head off, I thought. A Creole from New Orleans, indeed. If there's anyone in this building with Creole blood, it's me.

"I'm dying. Please help a dying widow ..." the voice wailed from the hall.

I unwillingly turned from the mirror. The Wig was perfection. Four-dollars-and-six-cents' worth of sheer art. The sacrifice had been worth it. I was reborn, purified, anointed, beautified.

"I'm just a poor helpless widow ..."

Would the bitch never shut up? With the majesty of a witch doctor, I went to Nonnie Swift's rescue.

She was sprawled on the rat-gnawed floorboards of the hall, clutching a spray of plastic violets, rhinestone Mother Hubbard robe spread out like a blanket under her aging, part-time-whore's body, which twitched rhythmically. Nonnie's blue-rinse bouffant was a wreck. It formed a sort of African halo. Tears sprang from her sea green contact lenses. She jerked Victorian-braceleted arms toward the ceiling and whimpered pitifully.

"What's wrong?" I asked.

Nonnie folded her arms across her pancake stomach and moaned.

I knelt down beside her, peered at her contorted rouged face, and got a powerful whiff of brandy.

Like a blind thief's, Nonnie's trembling hands pawed at my chin, nose, forehead, and The Wig.

I wanted to break her goddamned hand. "Don't mess with the moss," I said. "What's wrong with you?"

"I'm in great pain, Les."

I tried to lift her into a sitting position. The lower part of her body seemed anchored to the floorboards.

"Feel it," Nonnie said, belching.

"Feel what?"

"Feel it," Nonnie repeated tersely.

"Don't you ever give up? You're old enough to be my mother."

She screamed again. Cracked lips showed through her

American Lady lipstick, which is a deep, deep purple shade.

"Thank you, son," Nonnie sighed.

"Are you stoned?" I asked. I had a feeling she wasn't talking to me.

"Stoned?" Nonnie sneered. "I'm in *pain!*"

"Just try to sit up," I pleaded. "Then put your arm on the banister."

"What us poor women go through."

"Do you want me to call the doctor?"

"Yes! Call the doctor! Call the fire department! Call the militia!" Nonnie shouted. "It's coming. Two years over-due."

Disgusted, I stood up. "You're really loaded."

"I ain't no such thing. I've been trying to have this baby for a long time. I even said I'd have it on television. But they wouldn't let me. Of course *you* know why, don't you? I come from one of the oldest families in New Orleans, too. I'm only living among *you* people because of *him.* I want my son to see all the good and bad things in this world. Understand?"

I understood only too well. "Do you want me to help you to your pad?" I said. "I ain't got all day."

"You'd leave a pregnant woman flat on her back?"

Just then Mrs. Tucker opened her rusty tin-covered door. Resplendent in a pleated burlap sack dress and domed head, always sucking rotten gums, she stood and glared.

I glared right back. "Hey," I said. (That's Carolina talk for 'hello.') "Hey, you dried-up old midwife."

"Harlem riffraff," Mrs. Tucker spat. "A young punk and a common slut. You'd be lynched down home."

Nonnie raised up and said sweetly: "Mrs. Tucker, my baby is coming at last. Aren't you delighted?"

"A sin," Mrs. Tucker shuddered. She pulled her seventy-nine pounds up and slammed the tin-covered door.

"She just ain't friendly," Nonnie commented sadly.

"Don't let it get you down, cupcake."

"At least she could have offered to nurse my baby."

"Is the father a white man?"

"I hardly think so," Nonnie said slowly. "But you never can tell, can you?"

Suddenly, Nonnie was choked with sobs. Strong tears washed away the sea green contact lenses, leaving only the true color of her sky blue eyes. "No more pain, Les. I've paid the cost. But just think what he'll have to go through in Harlem. Leaving the warm prison of my womb. Born into unchained slavery."

I looked down at Nonnie. Perhaps she *was* Creole. "Things are getting better every day," I said.

"Oh. I hope so," Nonnie cried. "Things have got to change, or else I'll go back to my old mansion in the Garden District, where the weeds have grown and the Spanish moss just hangs and hangs, and the wind whistles through it like a mockingbird."

Does that chick read? I asked myself, can she? and decided probably not, she probably saw it and heard it all in the movies.

I had an urge to tell Nonnie she ought to be on the stage or in a zoo. I'd listened to all this fancy jazz for three years. I realize people have to have a little make-believe. It's like Mr. Fishback says: "Son, try it on for size because after you see me there'll be no more changes." Sooner or later, though, you have to step into the spotlight of reality. You've got to do your bit for yourself and society. I was trying for something real, concrete, with my Wig.

So I said to Nonnie, "I'm gonna make the big leap. I'm cutting out."

"You? Where the hell are you going?"

"Just you wait and see," I teased. "I'm gonna shake up this town."

"And just you wait and see," Nonnie mocked. "You curly-headed son of a bitch. You've conked your hair."

"Not conked," I corrected sharply. I wanted to give her a solid blow in the jaw and make her swallow those false teeth. "Just a little water and grease, Miss Swift."

"Conked."

"Do you want me to bash your face in?"

"I'm sorry, sweetcakes," Nonnie said.

"That's more like it. You're always putting the bad mouth on people. No wonder *you* people never get no-where. You don't help each other. You people should stick together like the gypsies."

"It's a pity, ain't it?"

Although I was fuming mad, I managed to lower my voice and make a plea for sympathy. "I can't help it if I have good hair. You can't blame a man for trying to better his condition, can you? I'm not putting on or acting snotty."

"I didn't wanna hurt your feelings," Nonnie said tearfully. "Honest, Les. You look sort of cute."

"Screw, baby."

"I really mean it. I hope my son has good hair. God knows he'll need something to make it in this world."

"That's a fact," I agreed solemnly. "The Wig is gonna see me through these troubled times."

Nonnie questioned the plastic violets for confirmation.

"It gives me a warm feeling to know that I can buy bread in my old age," she remarked with great dignity. "My baby boy will be a great something. I'm sure high school diplomas and college degrees are on the way out, now you can get them through the mail for a dollar ninety-eight, plus postage. Look at the mess all those degrees have got us in. By the time he's a grown man success might depend on something else. Might well be a good head of hair."

"That's true," I agreed. Then, blushing, I couldn't help but add: "You know, Nonnie, I feel like a new person. I know my luck is changing. My ship is just around the bend."

"I suppose so," Nonnie said bitchily. "I suppose that's the way you feel when your hair is conked."

I turned and began walking away. Otherwise, I would have strangled Nonnie Swift.

Now, she began to cry, to plead. "Les—Lester Jefferson. Don't leave me flat on my back. Please. I'm all alone. Mrs. Tucker won't help me. You'll have to sub for the doctor."

"Screw."

I had no time for the drunken hag. How could a New Orleans tramp appreciate The Wig? That's the way people are. Always trying to block the road to progress. But let me tell you something: no one, absolutely no one—nothing— is gonna stop this boy. I've taken the first step. All the other steps will fall easily into place.

Who was I talking to? Myself. Feeling at peace with myself and proud of my clear reasoning, I decided to make it up to Miss Sandra Hanover's on the third floor, to what Miss Sandra called her *pied-à-terre*.

Miss Sandra Hanover was intelligent, understanding. A lady with class.

TWO

The door, hung with an antique glass-beaded French funeral wreath, was open. Hopefully, I entered and looked over at Miss Sandra Hanover and was chilled to the bone.

Miss Sandra Hanover, ex–Miss Rosie Lamont, ex–Mrs. Roger Wilson, née Alvin Brown, needed a shave. The thick dark stubble was visible under two layers of female hormone powder. But she had plucked her eyebrows; they V'd up toward Chinese-style bangs like two frozen little black snakes. A Crown Princess, working toward a diva's cold perfection, she did not acknowledge my entrance. She looked silly as hell, sitting on a warped English down sofa, wearing a man's white shirt, green polka-dot tie, and blue serge trousers. Her eyes were closed and her Texas-cowboy sadist's boots morse-coded a lament. At home Miss Sandra Hanover normally wore a simple white hostess gown that she'd found in a thrift shop. So freakish, I thought, mustering up a smile.

Coming up, I'd decided not to comment on The Wig, realizing rhetoric would not be effective. The Wig would speak for itself, a prophet's message.

I went over to the warped sofa and said, "What's wrong?"

Miss Sandra Hanover clasped her two-inch fake-gold-fingernailed hands. Then she opened her bovine eyes, but made no reply.

"Did you upset those fagots last night?" I coaxed.

Miss Sandra Hanover blew her nose with a workman's handkerchief. Her face was bright. Then it caved. A chalice of tears.

"Oh, Les. It was simply awful. Remember Miss Susan Hayward in *I Wanna Live*?" Her voice was so heavy with suffering that I immediately thought of Jell-O.

"Yeah. But why the waterworks?"

The Crown Princess masked a doubting stare. She bolted over to the gun cabinet and got a perfumed Lily cigarette.

Imitating a high-fashion model's coltish stride, Miss Sandra Hanover paraded around the nine-by-seven *pied-à-terre,* striking grand bitchy Bette Davis poses.

Sucking in her breath, she suddenly stopped and began speaking as if she had rehearsed her monologue diligently:

"Well, I went to this drag party on Central Park West last night. Mr. Fishback couldn't chauffeur me in the Caddie. A night-rider funeral. So, your mother taxied down. Ever so grand. I looked like Miss Scarlett O'Hara. Miss Vivien Leigh was simply wonderful, wasn't she? You should have seen how lovely I looked, Les. Peach-colored satin. I let my silver foxes drag the floor like Miss Rita

Hayworth in *Gilda*. I'm maiding for this call girl on Sutton
Place South. The sweetest little thing from Arkansas. She
let me wear her diamond earrings like those Miss Audrey
Hepburn wore in *Breakfast at Tiffany's*. She had this John
glaze the foxes. The sweetest little furrier. I didn't even
have to do him. I just told him that he really loved his
mother. Like he wanted to sleep with her when he was
four years old."

"Still up to your old tricks." I laughed.

"Now, Lester Jefferson," Miss Sandra Hanover said
coyly. "Everybody's got *something* working for them. I bet
you've got something working for you."

Smiling and silent, I went and sat down in a modern
Danish chair that looked like a miniature ski lift.

Miss Sandra Hanover cleared her throat. "Remember
Miss Gloria Swanson in *Sunset Boulevard*? Coming down
that spacious staircase, mad with her own greatness,
beauty? And all those common reporters thinking she was
touched in the head? She knew deep down in her own
heart that she was a star of the first *multitude!* Well, love,
that was me last night."

Greedily relishing her victory, Miss Sandra Hanover
clucked her tongue, leaned back, and struck a *Vogue* pose.
Vigorous, in the American style, she wetted liver lips, exhaled, and continued: "Oh, did those fagots want to claw
my eyes out! I acted like visiting royalty. Remember Miss

Bette Davis in *Elizabeth and Essex*? I sat on that cockroach-
infested sofa like it was a throne and didn't even *dance!* I
just gave'm my great Miss Lena Horne smile …"

Drunk with dreams of glory, Miss Sandra Hanover's
voice became a coquette's confidential whisper: "Later,
things got out of hand. The lights were turned down low.
Sex and pot time. Miss Sammie knocked over the buffet
table, which was nothing but cold cuts anyway, and those
half-assed juvenile delinquents started fighting. I pressed
for the door.

"Three Alice Blue Gowns came running up the stoop.
Naturally, they thought I was a woman. I flirted like Miss
Ava Gardner in *The Barefoot Contessa.* Then this smart son-
of-a-bitch starts feeling me up. You see, I was a nervous
wreck dressing for the party. I couldn't find my falsies. I
looked high and low for those girls! I had to stick a pair of
socks in my bosom. And this smart-ass cop has a flashlight
and pulls out my brand-new Argyle socks. Oh! I was fit to
be tied. In high drag going to the can at two in the morning. Suffering like Miss Greta Garbo in *Camille,* and before
you knew it: daylight …"

"And the doll was ready for breakfast in bed," I joked,
craning my neck for a glimpse in the oval-shaped mirror
above Miss Hanover's crew cut.

She cleared her throat again and slumped back on the
sofa. "Breakfast? I couldn't eat a bit. Slop! I felt like Miss

Barbara Stanwyck in *Sorry, Wrong Number.* But I did this lovely guard and he brought me two aspirins and a cup of tea."

Miss Hanover fell silent. I couldn't resist another glance at myself in the mirror, dreaming an honest young man's dream: to succeed where my father had failed. Six-foot-five, 270 pounds, the exact color of an off-color Irishman, my father had learned to read and write extremely well at the age of thirty-six. He died while printing the letter Z for me. I was ten, and could offer my mother little comfort. I remember she sprayed the bread black. I remember the winter of my father's death as a period of black diamonds, for my mother and I had to hunt for coal that had fallen from trains along the railroad tracks. Like convicts hiding in an abandoned farmhouse, we sat huddled in our ram-shackle one room. My mother read to me by candlelight. I vowed that I would learn to write and read, to become human in the name of my father. The Wig wasn't just for kicks. It was rooted in something deeper, in the sorrow of the winter when I was ten years old.

Remembering this now, I bit my lower lip and turned to Miss Hanover. "It's a good day, doll."

But Miss Sandra Hanover only saw the blood of suffering. "Les, they sent me to a headshrinker. Everyone knows I'm a clever woman. I am *not* about to go to no nut ward! I lied to this closet queen. I said I was from down South and they'd told me it was all right to go in drag in 'Nue Yawk cit-tee.' The closet queen nodded her bald head and said, 'That's interesting.' 'Yes,' I smiled back like a nice little water boy. 'Don't feel bad. This is quite common among Negro homosexuals who come North.' 'Let's get this straight,' I said. 'I am *not* a homosexual. I am a real Negro woman.' 'You don't understand,' Miss Head-shrinker had the nerve to tell me. 'My name is Miss Sandra Hanover. Do you wanna see my ID card? You know. Blue is for boys and pink for girls.' Did Miss One turn red in the face! She excused herself and came back with two more closet queens. These bitches told me that I was a common Southern case. Ain't that a bitch? I was born and raised in Brooklyn. Now I got to take treatments twice a week because they think I is queer and come from the South. Why, everybody knows I'm a *white* woman from Georgia."

Miss Hanover leaned forward on the warped sofa and gestured like Mother Earth. Puckered liver lips. Her dark, aquiline nose quivered.

"Oh! I feel so bad. Remember how Miss Joan Crawford suffered so in *Mildred Pierce*? I could just die …"

A sharp intake of breath. A flurry of batting false eyelashes. A guttural sob, and Miss Sandra Hanover tumbled dramatically to the floor, very unladylike.

Dead she wasn't. No one like that ever dies. I got up,

found a bottle of Chanel No. 5, and bathed Miss Hanover's forehead and temples with the perfume.

Counting to ten, I stared at Miss Hanover's carefully brushed crew cut. I missed her glamorous false wig. It was true; everyone had something working for them.

Presently, the great actress regained consciousness.

Sighing erotically, she looked up at me. "I must have fainted. Isn't that strange? And you look strange too, love juice."

Swallowing hard, I backed toward the door. "I'd better be going," I said.

"Now, Les," Miss Hanover chided.

"I'll see you later, doll."

The Crown Princess rose quickly. "Come here, honey," she pleaded. "I ain't gonna bite you. My, my. Those beautiful curls. Naked, you'd look like a Greek statue."

"Yeah," I mumbled and bolted out the door and down to my second-floor sanctum. Pleasure, I reflected, was not necessarily progress, and I had a campaign to map out. I had to get my nerves together.

THREE

Whistling "Onward, Christian Soldiers," I put the night latch on my door. I wanted no one coming in. I lit a cigarette, flopped down on the landlord's hallelujah prize, a fire-damaged sofa bed, crossed my legs, and exhaled deeply. I smiled lightly, like a young man in a four-color ad. I realized that nothing is perfect, but still, there was a possibility I might now be able to breathe easier. The Wig's sneak preview could be called successful, provided one knew human nature. Nonnie Swift's taunts: pure jealousy. Miss Sandra Hanover: simply a case of lust. I grinned and touched my nose.

Dear Dead Mother and Father. Why do I have visions of guillotining you? Mother baked lemon pies. Father was a Pullman porter, a heroic man with a cat's gray eyes. Worthy colored serfs, good dry Methodists—they did not believe I had a future. How could they have possibly known? Otherwise, they'd have done something about my nose. No, it's not a Bob Hope nose, no one could slide down it, although it might make a plump backrest. If my parents had been farsighted, I would have gone to bed at night with a clothespin on my nose. At breakfast, Father would have peeped from behind the morning paper and lectured me on my bright future. (I've seen those damn ads and motion pictures. I know how fathers act at the breakfast table.)

Lord—just to think I could have had a sharp nose, a beak. However, in the morning? Yes, I said in the morning. In the afternoon. Yes, after the sun goes down, and I wanna tell you—at the crack of dawn. In the heat of summer or on a cold rainy day in November, and we all know about those dark days—when the sun refuses to shine. Yes. Sometimes there's no light in our souls. Yes, I wanna tell you—I can sweat until Judgment Day and no grease will run down my face. No grease will congeal behind my ears. My hair will not go "back home," back to the hearth of kinks and burrs. Silky Smooth is magnificent! I am no longer afraid. At last, I have a dog's sense of security. Yes.

I've seen my young Negro comrades downtown. Sharp as a son-of-a-bitch with their slick Silky Smooth hair. *Esquire* and *Gentlemen's Quarterly* have nothing on them. But as they approach Grand Central or Forty-second Street or Penn Station or Wall Street—they become as self-conscious as a sinner in church. Looking around the subway car nervously, clutching attaché cases. And just as the train approaches their station, out come the kinky-bur false wigs. And the others? The Buzz, Robin, Keith, Kipp, and Lance boys? The boys who can afford to be silky-smoothed twenty-four hours a day—Jim, you might as well forget it. These young men have "good" connections.

There is a very select shop in Harlem, on a side street.

The building is very old; it emits dust the way a human does when breathing hard. Quite often bricks fall from its façade and clobber pedestrians. Still, matrons of "good" Harlem families call the building Mecca.

I have memorized the discreet ad in the window of that building.

WE ARE AT LAST ABLE TO PROVIDE YOU PEOPLE WITH A COAT OF ARMS! DONE ENTIRELY BY IBM ON HEAVY, RAT-PROOF ANTIQUE PAPER. YOUR FAMILY NAME HAS BEEN CAREFULLY RESEARCHED FROM ALL THE PROPER BOOKS IN EXISTENCE. ONLY GOOD FAMILY NAMES ARE AVAILABLE—400— INCLUDING AFRICAN FAMILIES AS WELL AS THE COMMON NAMES FROM THE BRITISH ISLES.

Bewigged I am. Brave, an idealist. But what can I do without a good family name, a sponsor, a solid connection? There's Mr. Fishback but I'm not sure about Mr. Fishback. I have a funny feeling that one day, if you let Mr. Fishback help you, you'll have to pay up. In what way I can't say. But there'll be no way out.

Dammit! The doorbell buzzed, a desperate animal-like clawing, funny little noises, like a half-assed drummer trying to keep time.

Upset, I went and flung open the door.

Little Jimmie Wishbone stood there. A dusty felt hat

pulled down over his ears. Cracked dark glasses obscured his sultry eyes. The ragged Army poncho was dashing and faintly sinister, like a CIA playboy.

"Brroudder! Ain't you cracket up yet?" Little Jimmie shouted. "I thought I'd see you over thar."

I stiffened but gestured warmly. "Come in, man. When you get out?"

"Yestiddy, 'bout two o'clock."

"Good to see you, man."

Grunting like a hot detective, Little Jimmie surveyed the room. He flipped up the newspaper window shade and looked out on the twenty feet of rubbish in the backyard. He jerked open the closet curtains. Satisfied, he pulled a half-gallon of Summertime wine and Mr. Charlie's *Lucky Dream Book* from under the poncho and put them on the orange-crate coffee table.

"You're looking good," I said, hoping I didn't sound as if I were fishing for a compliment.

"Am I?" Little Jimmie wanted to know.

Sadly, I watched him ease down on the sofa bed, like a king in exile.

Aged twenty-eight, Little Wishbone was a has-been, a former movie star. *Adios* to fourteen Cadillacs, to an interest in a nationwide cathouse corporation. He had been the silent "fat" owner of seven narcotic nightclubs, had dined at the White House. Honored at a Blue Room homecoming reception after successfully touring the deep South *and*

South Africa. At the cold corn bread and molasses breakfast, Congressmen had sung "He's a Jolly Good Nigger."
Later, they had presented him with a medal, gold-plated,
the size of a silver dollar, carved with the figure of a naked
black man swinging from a pecan tree.

I had to hold back tears. Could that have been only two
years ago? I wondered. I got a couple of goblets from
under the dripping radiator. Mercy—depression multiplies
like cockroaches.

I couldn't look at him, so I pretended to polish the goblets with a Kleenex, remembering.

The NAACP had accused Hollywood of deliberately
presenting a false image of the American Negro. After the
scandal subsided, Little Jimmie had the privilege of
watching his own funeral. The government repossessed
his assets. The Attorney General wanted him jailed for
subversion but he pleaded insanity. Then his wife left him
for a rock 'n' roll bass-baritone and that really did send
him crazy. Little Jimmie had spent the past year commut-
ing between Kings County Hospital and Harlem, but he
had endured. The famed lamb's-wool hair had turned
white. Little Jimmie's gold teeth had turned purple. He
was slowly dying. Time and time again the doctors had
explained to him that Negroes did not have bleeding ulcers nor did they need sleeping pills. American Negroes,
they explained, were free as birds and animals in a rich
green forest. Childlike creatures, their minds ran the

gamut from Yes Sir to No Sir. There was simply no occasion for ulcers.

I poured a goblet of Summertime. Little Jimmie drank straight from the bottle.

"What's wrong?" he growled.

"Nothing, man."

"Something must be wrong," he insisted.

"What makes you say that?"

"'Cause something is wrong. You ain't ever drunk out of no glass like that before."

I blushed. "Oh. You mean ..."

"No. I don't mean. Hell. I got eyes. What you trying to prove?"

"You don't understand," I said sharply.

"Whacha trying to prove?"

"Whacha see? What's the impression? Slice the tater, slit the pea?"

In exactly one minute and three seconds, Little Jimmie had swallowed half of the wine. "Split the pea—I is with thee. What's the haps? Come clean. I is Little Jimmie Wishbone from Aukinsaw."

Brotherly love engulfed us. I drank from the bottle.

We had killed Summertime. Little Jimmie kept his eyes fastened on the empty wine bottle. He looked like an angelic little boy who had been kicked out of his orphanage for failing to take part in group masturbation.

"You look down," I said. "You need some nooky."

Little Jimmie sighed. He looked very tired. "Nooky? Dem white folk messed wit yo boy. Shot all dem currents through me. Y'all took way my libin', I said. And they jest kept shooting electricity. It was even popping out my ears. I took it like a champ. Kinda scared dem, too. I heard one of dem say: 'He's immune. It's the result of perpetual broilization. Nothing will ever kill a Nigger like this.' I did my buck dance and the doctor said, 'They got magic in their feet.' Man, I danced into the village. Now they can't figure out why those currents and saltpeter make me so restless. They puzzled. I'm amused. But it's not like my Hollywood days. All my fans and those lights and twenty-seven Cadillacs."

"Fourteen Cadillacs," I corrected.

"Fourteen," Little Jimmie agreed. "But I traded them in every year. Les, I just don't feel right. I just ain't me."

"I know what you mean."

"What am I gonna do?"

"You need another drink."

"Yeah. Some juice. Out there …"

"You didn't escape, did you?"

"Where could I escape to?" Little Jimmie exclaimed.

"Nowhere, man," I said, averting my eyes.

"I can't even get unemployment, though I was honorary president of the Screen Guild."

"You could always pick cotton in Jersey," I said.

"Pick cotton?" Little Jimmie sneered. "What would my fans think? I think I'll appeal to the Supreme Court. I

33

figure they owe me an apology. I worked for the government, man. I kept one hundred million colored people contented for years. And in turn, I made the white people happy. Safe. Now I'm no longer useful in the scheme of things. Nobody's got time for Little Jimmie Wishbone."

"What did you expect? Another medal? It's not profitable to have you *Tom* ... It's a very different scene."

"Well, what are you gonna do? Why the hell don't *you* pick cotton?"

"What the hell do you think I was doing last summer? *Where* do you think I got the money for the fried chicken I brought you on Sundays?"

War between friends is deadly. I mustered up a breathless laugh. "I'm gonna try something I never tried before. Dig The Wig."

Little Jimmie grunted scornfully. "Look at all those curly-haired Mexicans they import to pick berries and cabbage."

"But I'm an American," I protested.

"And I've got a million dollars."

"I *am* an American. That's an established fact. America's the land of elbow grease and hard work. Then you've got it made. Little Jimmie, I'm gonna work like a son of a bitch. Do you hear me?"

"Yeah. I heard you. Now let's make it to the streets. My throat's dry."

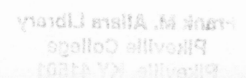

FOUR

Little Jimmie and I moved out into the street under a volcanic gray sky. A cold wind made a contradictory hissing like an overheated radiator, crept under heavy clothing with a shy but determined hand. Nothing could stifle our sense of adventure; Little Jimmie was home again, and I always feel cocksure, Nazi-proud, stepping smartly toward the heart of Harlem—125th Street.

One Hundred and Twenty-fifth Street has grandeur if you know how to look at it. Harlem, the very name a part of New World History, is a ghetto nuovo, on the Hudson; it reeks with frustrations and an ounce of job. Lonely, I often leave my airless room on Saturday night, wander up and down 125th Street, dreaming of making it, dreaming of love. This is the magical hour. The desperate daytime has, for a time, disappeared. The bitter saliva puddles of the poor are covered with sperm, dropped by slumming whites and their dark friends who wallow in the nightclubs that go on to early morning. These are people who can afford to escape the daytime fear of the city. Envious, I watch their entrances and exits from the clubs. I especially watch the Negroes, who pretend that the black-faced poor do not exist.

I glanced at my misbegotten friend, a silent but bright-eyed Little Jimmie Wishbone. In his heyday, he'd been unique: a real person, an offbeat hero. Now he was only a confused shadow.

"Look where we are," I cried out as we swung on to East 125th Street.

Little Jimmie grunted. "What's playing at the Apollo? I once had a one-night stand at the Apollo and they held me over for six weeks."

"I remember. You were great. Man, listen to that wind!"

"The Apollo is show biz uptown."

"Yeah," I said quickly. "Man. The wind is a mother grabber. I really need some joy-juice."

"The Apollo is the last outpost. No other place like it in Manhattan."

I began whistling "Them There Eyes"—a nervous habit of mine. Diplomatic phrases refused to slide off my tongue. Presently, Little Jimmie would see the legendary Apollo Theater, its lobby a bower of plastic out-of-season flowers, shuttered and forlorn, due to the management's judgment (bad) in booking a string quartet from South Africa. This had shocked the entire city. The Mayor held a press conference. Harlemites stayed home in their photogenic tenements and watched television travelogues of Southern hospitality, while a group of near-naked white liberals picketed the Apollo. They mourned the loss of Negro music—so powerful that one felt it in the soles of one's feet (if one did not truly feel it, then one visited a chiropodist). The liberals prayed for a soul-shaking orgy. After three days, they marched back downtown, bewailing the Negroes' torpid attitude.

Gradually an aura of commerce, peace, splendor returned to 125th Street. Blumstein's Department Store announced in the *Amsterdam News* that polar-bear rugs were obsolete. Human-hair rugs were the latest rage. These rugs, clipped from live Negro traitors, had a lifetime guarantee. Blumstein's reported a remarkable sale. The Society of American Interior Decorators declared human-hair rugs "in." And the Du Pont Empire closely watched the proceedings. If human-hair rugs became a truly basic part of the American Home, perhaps they'd produce them in synthetics.

Strolling briskly with my friend, I felt pride seep into my pores. I was part of this world. The Great White Father had spoken. His white sons were carrying out his word. His black flunkies were falling in line. The opportunity for Negroes to *progress* was truly coming. I could hear a tinkling fountain sing: "I'll wash away your black misery— *tum-tiddy-diddy-tum-tee-tee.*" Yes. Wigged and very much aware of the happenings, I knew my ship was just around the bend, even as I had informed Miss Nonnie Swift.

One Hundred Twenty-fifth Street, with its residential parks, its quaint stinking alleys, is a sea of music, Georgian chants, German lieder, Italian arias, Elizabethan ballads. Arabic lullabies, lusty hillbilly tunes. Negro music is banned except for propaganda purposes. "We'll let *them* borrow our music," a Negro politician remarked recently. "We'll *see* what it does for them. We'll see if *they* ride to glory on our music." I remember the Negro politician sailed a week later on a yacht, a sparkling-white yacht, complete with sauna, wine cellar, and a stereo record collection of Negro music second only to the Library of Congress's.

No one's perfect, I was thinking, when Little Jimmie elbowed me.

"I see *they're* still here," he said angrily.

"Of course, Little Jimmie," I said softly, mindful of his mental condition, his swift descent from Fame.

"You're nuts."

"Don't get yourself worked up," I said. "No one's gonna bother you."

"But they're still here," Little Jimmie protested.

"Naturally." I knew all along what had him bugged. It was the police.

New York's finest were on the scene, wearing custommade Chipp uniforms, 1818 Brooks Brothers shirts, Doctor U space shoes (bought wholesale from a straw basket in Herald Square). A pacifistic honor guard, twelve policemen per block, ambitious nightsticks trimmed with lilies of the valley, we are our brother's keeper buttons illuminating sharp-brimmed Fascist helmets—they bow to each fast-moving Harlemite from crummy Lenox to jet-bound Eighth Avenue.

Little Jimmie's fear was disgusting. The policemen were

our protectors, knights of the Manhattan world. I wasn't afraid. I was goddam grateful.

"Are you ready?" I asked cheerfully.

Little Jimmie groaned deeply. "Lord. I might as well be back in Kings County's nut ward."

"It ain't that bad."

"That's your story, morning glory. It wasn't bad when I was riding through like Caesar in my bullet-proof Caddie ..."

"You have got to get used to the streets again. That's all. Doesn't it feel good to be home again?"

"I suppose so," Little Jimmie said slowly. "I guess I been away too long."

"Everything's still the same," I told him. "We're very fortunate to live in a ghetto that still honors traditional values."

Little Jimmie motioned across the street. "What's that funny-looking little green house over there?"

"That's an electronic snake pit. When things get too tough, you just hold this electronic cord until you can't stand it any longer. A gas. Almost like taking dope. Cheaper than the subway."

"It jest don't seem like Harlem any more."

"But this is home, baby! This is the only place in the world where you can have the time of your life. You always could, and we still do."

"That's why I'm scared," Little Jimmie said.

"But it's different now," I tried to explain. "Even the cops are different."

"I don't hear a word you're saying."

I tried to reassure Little Jimmie, brushing back a curly lock that rose in the wind, which whipped through the skeleton of an apartment house fringing a condemned residential park. "The cops are our friends."

"Then why do we have to run?"

"You'll never understand," I said, sighing. "Are you ready?"

"Give me a head start," Little Jimmie whined.

"Why do you want a head start?"

"Didn't they give you a medal last year 'cause the bloodhounds couldn't catch you?"

"Jesus. I'd almost forgotten. I guess I'm sort of an American hero."

"Yeah, and I've always been a movie star. But give me a head start. I've been taking the waters at Kings County."

"We gotta make it just to Eighth Avenue. It's not like a cross-country race."

"It's the same!" Little Jimmie cried. He pulled the felt hat down over his ears and started off.

I let him have a comfortable lead. Arching my arms, head held high, I bounded off graciously, the son of a desperate, dead runner.

Up ahead, a policeman sharpening a bowie knife snapped to attention as I dashed across Lenox Avenue.

Bowing, the policeman said, "Good morning, sir."

"Morning," I replied, gasping for breath. I'd never been frightened before, believe me. Little Jimmie's gloomy forecast, I told myself. He's a very sick has-been.

And soon I bypassed him, smoothly sprinting toward a photo finish. I galloped across the right side of Eighth Avenue, feeling my ego-oats. I was in good condition for the Spring Run-Nigger-Run track meet (the winner of this meet receives a dull black wrought-iron Davis Cup. There is always savage bribery; each Borough President shills and makes a play for his favorite black son). Sunrise, sunset, winter, or summer—it had never been Succoth—the Promised Land, or the ingathering of the harvest for me. But with The Wig it might soon be.

I wiped my sweaty brow and saw three whores standing on the corner, adjusting white kid gloves.

"Little Jimmie," I called. "Look at our reward. Standing tall, sweet, and brown."

Little Jimmie eased up his pained physical-fitness smile. "Call the mojo man. Too bad Caddie number twenty is in the repair shop."

Stalking coolly, we approached the three whores.

I opened. "What you pretty girls doing out in this weather?"

The finely built group spokesman scanned the sky and giggled. "We're waiting on the Junior League pick-up truck. Those fine ladies, always so discriminating, have consented to see us. We're gonna add a little funky color to their jaded lives. Ain't that nice? They're planning a tea benefit for Harlem settlement houses. We're in charge of the entertainment. Ain't that nice?"

"It sure is," Little Jimmie guffawed boyishly.

"An honor," I agreed, eyeing the innocent, lyrically pretty debutante. Tawny, a smasher, she toyed with short white gloves and averted her dark bacon-and-eggs eyes.

I remained worldly, indifferent, like Marcello Mastroianni. Then, to change the pace, I grinned a Humphrey Bogart grin.

Spongecake number two cleared her throat. "Well, well. I do declare."

"You look sort of familiar," the group spokesman said to Little Jimmie.

The rusty gates of glory creaked open; Little Jimmie cocked his hat on the back of his head and said in a resonant voice: "I jest might be. I is Little Jimmie Wishbone from Aukinsaw."

The group spokesman clutched a gloved hand over her right tit. "Little Jimmy Wishbone, the movie star? Oh, I feel faint!"

"I do declare," Spongecake said. "I heard you were on skid row."

"That was only for a proposed television series," Little Jimmie said modestly.

The whores feigned belief. Little Jimmie beamed. I blushed, watching three spotted horses trot toward the Harlem Premium Priceless meat factory. My stomach grumbled. I hadn't eaten in two days due to my extravagant Silky Smooth act.

"When you gonna make another picture like *Southern Sunset?*" the group spokesman asked in matronly tones.

"Well," Little Jimmie began grandly, "My old company, MGM, wants to sign me up for a Western epic. But my agent warned we'd better be incorporated in Switzerland first. I'm a hot property, you know."

The group spokesman gave her fellow travelers a firm didn't-I-tell-you-so expression. "A comeback, girls. A surefire sellout benefit première. I must inform our ticket scalpers."

"Hollywood is very excited over Little Jimmie's comeback," I said.

"I do declare," Spongecake said.

The calculating charm of the finely built, matronly spokesman began to show. "Which direction might you be headed, Mr. Wishbone?"

Little Jimmie shrugged, basking in the glow of the past. "Me and my boy jest out for a bit of fresh air."

"You and your valet?" Spongecake asked. "I read about your servants in *Screen Horror.*"

"I got him in Hong Kong last year."

"I do declare."

I wanted to kill the dirty, wine-drinking son of a bitch. I bowed my beautiful head in shame, silently vowing to see Madam X, the reincarnation of Medusa, the smoldering rage of the Harlem firmament. A few incantations by her, and Little Jimmie's wagon would really be fixed.

"Orientals make the best servants," the spokesman commented.

"That's true," Little Jimmie was quick to agree. In Hollywood, he'd had a Finnish cook and a British gentleman's gentleman.

"We're servantless. Thursday, you know," the spokesman smiled sweetly. "And we're simply delighted to meet you, Mr. Wishbone, in the flesh. I think we should give those Junior League girls a rain check. Another day for dice and cards and chitchat and Bloody Marys. But I'd be delighted if you'd join me in my study for an informal lunch. I'm a follower of Dione Lucas and James Beard, you know. I'll try to whip up something simple. Kale and turnip greens cooked with juicy ham hocks. Yankee pot roast. German potato salad. Green beans soaked in fat back. And my specialty, cornbread and sweet-potato pie."

Little Jimmie made a dapper bow. Lordly he said, "Delighted. One gets tired of frozen frog legs, frozen cornish hen, instant wild rice, and pasteurized caviar."

"Well, just come along with us," Hostess spokesman

smiled. "The Deb can stay with your valet and keep him
company. 'Bout as close to royalty as she'll ever get."

Swooning, Spongecake said: "I do declare. Such a refreshing change from the round of parties and balls and
dinners at the Bath club where we're always encountering
the same crowd."

The worms in my stomach were too hurt to cry over the
great luncheon—they were resigned.

I watched spokesman and Spongecake proudly encircle
Little Jimmie, saunter down Eighth Avenue.

"And you have twenty-five Caddies," Spongecake mar-
veled.

"Forty-two," Little Jimmie lied. "And I'm getting a Rolls
next week."

A loner, always on the outside, I looked at The Deb.

"You sure got pretty hair," she said.

"You really think so?" I asked, ready to assume my
lover-boy role.

She nodded. I could see her body tremble under her
battered tweed windbreaker. "My hair is so short and
kinky. Nobody wants me."

Silly girl. Poor, innocent, and good—Lord, a piece of
my lonely heart and hot hands telepathically grabbed her
bosom. We were on the same wavelength.

"Everybody wants you," I said. "You're lovely."

"No," The Deb cried. "I've got bad hair. I've tried

Madam C.J. Walker and Lady Clairol too. Oh, I don't know how I can go on living."

I went over and put my arms around her. She moaned and fell into them easily.

Yes. The touch of her flesh made lizards scale through my body as on sun-scorched rocks. I had never felt such sweet desire and I was grateful for the power and glory of The Wig.

"You're ever so kind," The Deb whispered. "All foreign men are real gentlemen."

Despite icy winds, sweat trickled down my armpits. It was the first time I'd been called a gentleman. "Oh, I wouldn't say that."

"It's true. Every time a Swedish ship comes to town I feel like the Queen of Sheba. And you're a man of quality. So sensitive. I can feel it."

"You're a sweet little thing" I murmured, feeling rather Swedish myself.

"You're ever so kind."

"Let's make it, baby. Some place that has a view, an open fire, soft lights, and sweet music."

"It sounds so romantic," The Deb cried, her lips brushing against my chin. "But how much you gonna pay me?"

"What?"

"How much you gonna pay me for my charms. You know: money. Loot. Bread. Greenback dollar bills."

"In Europe," I stammered, "we believe in free love ..."

"This ain't Europe, honey. This is New York City. You gotta pay one way or the other. I'm a simple cash-and-carry girl."

She elbowed my chest and broke away.

"You American females are very strange. In Europe ..."

"Sweetie, I dig you *and* your Wig. But they'd bar me from the union if I gave it away. The chairman said: 'No finance, no romance.' I hope you understand."

Sadly, I slumped against a litter basket. I'd had The Wig less than four hours and already I felt the black clouds gathering.

"I'll see you around, sweetie," The Deb smiled and walked away.

"Yeah," I mumbled, comforted with the knowledge that I was at least on the right side of Eighth Avenue.

FIVE

Rejected, dejected, I started walking east on 125th Street. The wind was dying and the sun had come out. Those cool knights, the cops, were dozing or filing their fingernails or reading newspapers. Negroes no longer raced across streets. They had slowed to a sensual stride. It was siesta time in Harlem. Everything was so quiet and peaceful that you wanted to take the mood home in a paper bag and sleep with it.

A candy store's loudspeaker played a Bach sonata—Landowska on the harpsichord. But the only music I heard was "no finance, no romance." The Deb, I sighed, feeling my whole body shake like thunder.

Up ahead loomed a great big fat bank, a foreign bank. Bracing my shoulders, I went into the bank and asked about a porter's job. I might as well try the dream of working my way up. Yes, there was an opening, I was informed by a very polite Negro girl with strawberry-blond hair. First, I had to fill out an application and take a six weeks' course in the art of being human, in the art of being white. The fee for the course would be one-five-o.

I thanked the girl with a weak smile, saying I'd return later in the afternoon or perhaps tomorrow. I'd have to place a long-distance call to Nassau.

"My father's in Nassau," I added, "Hitting the golf balls right down the middle. He's dead set on Yale, but I like to build my own roads."

Outside, in the quiet street, I saw a crowd gathering and went over. A Negro Civil Service worker—he looked to be about forty-five—had dropped dead. His skin had turned purple blue-black.

"Oh, Lord," a woman cried, gesturing like a fishwife in an Italian movie. "I'm a widow and my husband is dead. All his life, he'd wanted to go to Florida in the wintertime, when the snow's on the ground in New York. All his life he'd wanted that. And we were going next week. Oh, Lord. He'd been having these heart attacks caused by terrible racial nightmares ..."

A worldly looking young Negro couple next to me whispered: "It's a publicity stunt. The dead joker aped those Buddhist monks who used to set fire to themselves."

"Jesus," I shuddered and then began running, running home. Suddenly frightened, knowing if I didn't swing a secure gig, twenty years from now, I'd be flat on my own back, my chafed lips open as if to receive a slice of honeydew melon. Purple blue-black and dead, spotlighted by the early afternoon sun.

Darkness, symbol of life, arrived. I was naked and alone, clutching a patched gray sheet, lamenting The Wig's first encounters with destiny.

But there was the fat-back sensation of meeting The Deb, and the glorification of what I had always referred to privately as "my thorny crown," The Wig itself. I turned uneasily on the sofa bed, wary of the night guard of cockroaches. "Happy Days Are Here Again," I whistled softly, thinking of The Wig and trying to make myself feel good and then, Lord—my own private motion picture flashed on: memory.

I remembered Abraham Lincoln, who had died for me. I remembered the Negro maid who had walked from Grapetree, Mississippi, to Cold Spring Harbor, Long Island, and was flogged for being too maidenly fair. I remembered the young man who, competing for the title "Blacker the Berry, Sweeter the Juice," was killed during an avant-garde happening in a Washington Mews carriage house. The killing did *not* take place during a Black Mass, as was first reported. The Negro youth had committed a sexual outrage, according to *Confidential Magazine* in its exclusive interview with the host and hostess, who were famous for their collection of Contemporary Stone Art. Their sexual safaris were legendary, too. Inspired by childhood tales of lynchings (ah, the gyrations, the moans, the sweat, the smell of fresh blood, the uncircumcised odor), the couple had explored Latin rice-and-bean delights, European around-the-world-scootee-roots, Near Eastern lamb, flip-flop, and it's-all-in-the-family.

Hoping to avoid the press, which arrived by helicopter,

fifty miles from shore, exhausted, jaded, they returned to their native land on a luxury liner but in steerage class, with seventy pieces of Louis Vuitton luggage.

"It was off-season," the hostess had jokingly told reporters. The host added with great dignity: "We are returning to our native land, where fornication is pure and simple. We're returning to the womb of nature." They went into seclusion in their Greenwich Village carriage house until the night of the celebrated "happening," the night that was to reestablish their worldly reputation. The gleaming, white-toothed young Negro with the rough but carefully combed kinky hair (if one ran one's hand through his hair, one trembled and saw Venus and Mars) displayed a rosebud instead of a penis! The effrontery—a Negro and nipped in the bud! Certainly a shock that could drive anyone to murder, only it hadn't been murder, the courts decided. It was only a happening.

Sleepless still, I rolled over and scratched my stomach. I felt weak—a sure sign that happy days were here again and that I'd already opened a new door. As a child I'd always believed I could fly. One night, after sniffing The Big O in someone's bathroom, I *knew* it was possible. Until the countdown. Then I couldn't stand up, I was anchored to the floorboards. But the sensation, the idea of flight, the sensation of being free, that had been wonderful! I touched The Wig. Yes. Security had always eluded me, but

it wouldn't much longer. American until the last breath, a
true believer in The Great Society, I'd turn the other cheek,
cheat, steal, take the fifth amendment, walk bare-assed up
Mr. Jones's ladder, and state firmly that I was too human.

Lying in the quiet darkness, I decided to see Little Jimmie in the morning and work on a new big-time money-
making deal. But first, we'd have an early morning séance
with The Duke.

Yes! This was the land of hope and that was it! Sweet
brown girl, I'll become a magician for you. Sweet brown
girl. Bulldozing between your thighs, you with roses in
your hair, I thought as my eyelids grew heavy.

No. No, no!

Sleep. Dream. Rest in peace. Until morning.

2

"IF I COULD HOLLER LIKE A MOUNTAIN JACK ..."

—from JOE WILLIAMS SINGS

SIX

We kept our early morning séance with The Duke. He'd come a long way from his handyman-porter days in Chicago. A perfect specimen of the young man on the Amen train to success, the Duke had recently returned from his forty-seventh expedition into the Deep South and he had returned with a fantastic collection of antiques, a rare, historic collection. Sincere culture-prowling clubwomen were bursting out of their Edith Lances bras, trying to persuade The Duke to let his collection be included on their spring house tours.

The collection was extraordinary. It included the last word in expensive water hoses (nozzles intact, brassy but dented by human skulls); an enormous hunk of chestnut-colored hair from a Georgia policeman's gentle dog (The Duke planned to have this among his contemporary masterpieces); a hand-carved charred cross seven feet long; three dried Florida black snakes in a filigree shadow box; a lace handkerchief, reputed to be one of the oldest in America. These assorted objects were casually arranged in The Duke's mansion on the solid gilt edge of Central Park North and Fifth Avenue.

Little Jimmie and I swanked our way toward the Avenue. I saw people shield their eyes from The Wig.

"It's another world when the sun is shining," I remarked, but Little Jimmie made no answer.

Little Jimmie was in another world, very serious. Elegant: a twelve-foot cashmere striped old school scarf boa'ed his neck. Pigskin-gloved hands clutched a clear plastic attaché case bulging with ancient rock 'n' roll music he'd acquired at the Parke-Bernet galleries.

"What we gonna do first?" he asked solemnly.

"I don't know. Let's hope The Duke has some good stuff. Let's hope it inspires us. How's the lips?"

"I can't hang'm any lower, Les."

"At least you could try. This is very important, you know."

"No, I can't," Little Jimmie insisted. "Hollywood couldn't do anything with my patrician lips. The make-up man, and he was an artist to his fingertips, finally gave up."

"But we're rock 'n' roll singers," I tried to explain. "We've got to *dum-dee-dum*. You know, American kids are flipping over anything that has a jungle sound. It's their coming-of-age ritual."

Little Jimmie stopped suddenly. "Didn't have nothing like that when I was growing up. Didn't have nothing but misery and floggings."

"I know," I said, tugging gently at his arm. We were approaching the stark splendor of Central Park North, where green leaves were in embryo, and I wanted to get Little Jimmie to The Duke's.

"Kids got it too good now," he complained. "TV, bubble gum, plenty to eat. Nothing bad ever happens to them except they die from an overdose of heroin or else they go to jail for shooting a cop or a cop shoots them to an early grave. Yeah. Kids got it too good now."

"But their new way of life is our gravy. If they didn't dig rock 'n' roll and weren't so goddam queer we wouldn't be on our way to fame and fortune."

"That's right," Little Jimmie finally agreed. "Where's The Duke's pad?"

"See that manse on the left-hand side of the street?" I asked proudly. "The manse with the orange-tasseled canopy?"

"You mean the one that looks like that leaning tower in Italy?"

"That's it. Ain't that manse saying something? Something right out of *House and Garden*?"

"Oh, it's a mother-grabber. But I had thirty-five Caddies and I hear The Duke's only got one coup-de-ville Caddy and that's almost a year old. I used to trade my Caddies in every four months."

Little Jimmie slowed, deep in past memories.

"Sure," I said, and, tugging his arm, I led him gently across the street.

The Duke's soot-caked five-and-a-half-story limestone

mansion did lean slightly out over the sidewalk, but, as he once remarked, that was part of its charm. It was a real conversation piece. Who else in Manhattan could boast that half of the fifth floor had fallen into the street by itself? The Duke didn't even have to call the demolition crew, though the Sanitation Department complained like hell when they had to clean up the bodies of three small children, all victims of rickets disease. A joyous Welfare Department sent The Duke a twenty-five-year-old quart of Scotch and officially axed the children from their list. The poor mother, The Duke had told me with tears in his eyes, was twenty-three and very frail and had seven other illegitimate children on welfare, including two sets of twins.

"It's a beauty," Little Jimmy exclaimed as we bounced up the gold-veined marble steps. "But in my Hollywood heyday I had a twenty-car garage. Miss Mary Pickford and Mr. Douglas Fairbanks, Senior, ruled Hollywood in the twenties and *I* ruled Hollywood after the Second World War. That is, until those devils sent me into exile ..."

Little Jimmie shed one great tear, his trembling hand grasped the railing of the stoop.

"Now, don't go into that again," I said softly. "You'll get upset and be back in Kings County. Everything's cool. You're gonna reap fame and fortune in another field."

"But I was a star," Little Jimmie protested. "A movie star is the greatest thing in the world. A movie star lives forever."

I nodded and pressed the buzzer. The Wig would live

forever, I thought. A monument to progress in the name of my dead parents.

Presently, the double-barred iron door swung open and we went into the bare white entrance hall.

Brandishing a genuine poison bow and arrow, The Duke emerged from behind a sackcloth curtain. Exactly five-foot-five, a dark version of Maximilian of Mexico, he carefully wrapped the bow and arrow in several back issues of *The National Review*. He wore bright Turkish trousers and a Hong Kong patchwork smoking jacket.

"Adds a little color to my life," he joked. "I was afraid you boys wouldn't show."

"What made you think that?" I asked. "After all, we got big deals brewing."

"Well," The Duke began, "you know how it is. People are discovering that marijuana is bad for the teeth."

"I've heard," Little Jimmie said sadly.

"However," I said, putting mountain air and clear running springs into my voice, "What pot does for the intellect and the soul! And you get high, too. Getting high is gonna see me through this world."

"I know," The Duke said, displaying a garland of black teeth stumps. "Marijuana is habit-forming, like hatred. It's being reclassified as a major drug by the government ..." The Duke paused and rubbed his soft hands together. "What will it be today, boys?"

"I guess you heard," I said blushing.

"Oh. You mean ... The Wig. It's great, man."

"Just a little experiment. Taking a public poll, you might say. And then I'll get down to the heart of the matter."

Little Jimmie grunted. "He looks like a goddam Christmas tree. Blinding everybody on the street. There was a terrific traffic jam at 125th. Six people injured, but they was all white."

"Didn't I say I was going to shake up this town?" I laughed.

"Well," The Duke nodded in agreement, "I don't see how you can fail."

"I never needed a wig," Little Jimmie boasted. "But I was a movie star of the first rank. The late Louis B. Mayer said, 'Little Jimmie, you and I keep the lion roaring here at MGM." And I said, 'That's a fact, Louis.'"

"I remember," The Duke said quickly. "Nobody could touch you with a ten-foot pole until you lost your place as America's favorite dark Mickey Rooney."

"I never lost my place in the American moviegoer's heart," Little Jimmie cried. He flung the plastic attaché case to the floor angrily. "It was those secret devils that double-crossed me ..."

"What secret agents?" I scoffed, forgetting that he was touched in the head.

"How should I know?" Little Jimmie pleaded. "All I know is I'd jest been made an honorary member of the Arm Forces. This was wartime, mind you, but General Motors okayed a custom-built job for me. I was essential to the war effort. I made the people on the home front forget fear and tragedy."

Lies, insanity—I didn't care. "Peace on the home front? What the hell are you talking about? There was tragedy. My father learned to read and write and then died. My mother died grieving over him. That's how things were then. And I suppose you showed your teeth when the white folks said, 'Two more niggers gone.' I remember in the picture called *The Educated Man* there was a line that made the whole country laugh. 'No sur. Me caint weed nor wight to save muh name ...'"

Little Jimmie came over and tried to console me. "That was just part of the script, Les."

"Then why did you always sign your name with a rubber stamp and put an *X* beside it?"

"That was a gimmick. I had a good public relations working for me."

"But do you really know how to read and write?" I asked, breaking away from his grasp.

"I know how to read the Gallup Poll, *Variety,* and *The Hollywood Reporter.* I placed first in *Photo Digest Magazine's* popularity contest five years in a row. And then ..."

Little Jimmie slumped against the wall and moaned, head hung low; large, ashy hands grasping at something that wasn't there.

The Duke sighed. I felt a quick pain, felt sweat splash

down my armpits. I thought of The Wig and my own daz-
zling future, but that brought little comfort now.

Finally I forced myself to say loud and clear: "Yeah. Just
about the time you were gonna get an Academy Award
they kicked your ass out of Hollywood."

Little Jimmie raised his head slowly and looked over at
me. "You didn't have to say it like that, Les."

"What else could I say? It's the truth. It wasn't my fault
the white goat had horns."

The Duke broke in sweetly: "I've got some good stuff
for you colored rock 'n' roll singers. Colored rock 'n' roll
singers. That's a laugh. Sure you boys ain't trying to go
white on me? Anyway, you're in my corner. I've got quality stuff. A five- or ten-dollar bag?"

"We'll have a couple of joints and turn on and see what
happens. Okay, Little Jimmie?"

"I don't care. New gig shaping up and you guys trying
to put me down." He smiled painfully.

"Go ahead, baby. Plough through the rye," I said, following The Duke into the next room.

It was an L-shaped room with what had once been a
dumbwaiter converted into a drug bar. When The Duke
moved in, he had discovered a dead, half-Seal Point, half-
Abyssinian cat whose sky blue eyes now floated in a
Mason jar of alcohol. Functioning as a free-form shelf, a
colonial pine packing case sagged under the weight of

Chinese canisters (the pattern designs were the bonus of instant Australian tinned beef). A large, Danish cut-glass bowl was a rich sea of marijuana, finely chopped, heavily seeded, and blended for flavor and its dried-leaf color.

"Everything's in marvelous taste," I said.

"Yeah," Little Jimmie agreed.

"Thank you," The Duke smiled, and let us on into his private sitting room, a mild gray room, bare except for the seven-foot charred cross opposite a modern sofa. The Duke did not want people to miss the significance of the cross. Posters of the Nazi epoch, the Spanish Civil War, four-color spreads of winters at Miami Beach, and one discreet calling card from a family in Newport surrounded the cross.

"Gentlemen," The Duke said graciously, "I am at your service."

Little Jimmie flopped down on the sofa. He seemed not to notice the cross.

I sat down on a hassock made from a four-gallon tin of Muddy Blue detergent, a souvenir of The Duke's handyman-porter days.

The Duke was a fine host. Calmly, he offered Little Jimmie a brimming Malacca pipe of pot.

I already had my hand out for the fat rolled joint. I lit up, inhaled deeply, and thought: Happy days. Little Jimmie and I will be rock 'n' roll sensations. Plus, I have The Wig;

plus, there is still potency in the Little Jimmie Wishbone name. Plus, pot.

Feeling the pot and my bravado load, I went to the drug bar and flipped another joint into my golden lips and then looked over at Little Jimmie.

"Another pipe, man?"

Holding the pot in his head, riffling sheet music, Little Jimmie nodded gravely and I refilled his pipe.

Dry-heaving, The Duke clamped his hands over his mouth and turned toward the wall.

Two minutes later, he swung back around, breathing hard. "Fill my sax, Les. We'll make a session."

The Duke, a frustrated musician, always smoked pot out of a baby saxophone. A cute gimmick, like those coffee-house musicians before Lily Law ended that scene. Smoke drifting out of the saxophone, a motif of cool music.

I filled the sax and joined The Duke, who now sat Indian fashion on the floor.

Three (pot-smoking) Wise Men, we silently savored the joy of marijuana, unmoved by the 10 A.M. foghorns signaling the first quarterly hour of radioactive dust.

The Duke elbowed me. "Are you feeling it?" he grinned.

"I am getting together," I replied. The image of The Deb floated into my mind. Boiling with inspiration, I added: "We could start off with a rock 'n' roll love song."

You upset me like the subway at night
Do, do, do uh a do ... do
We'll hold hands in the first car
You and I and Oh ...
Do, do, do, uh a do the policeman.
Do, do, do, uh a do, do.

"What's the rest of it?" Little Jimmie asked.

"That's all. We jest keep repeating. Then let the sax and piano pick it up and, baby, we have at least two minutes. A record. A hit on our hands. By the time we make our first personal appearance on a TV show, we'll think of something freakish. You've gotta have something freakish about your personality or else the kids won't dig you. We gotta provide fantasy for their wet dreams."

The Duke exhaled and cleared his throat. "I think you're barking up the wrong tree. We're moving into a very *brotherly* racial era. And what's bringing the colored and white people together is real soul music. You know that, Les."

"Funky," Little Jimmie Wishbone shouted. "After the pot and whiskey, everything is jest like yesterday. And there's no real music. When I was a movie star ..."

"But listen," The Duke interrupted. He knifed up from the floor. The sax rested easily under his arm. You could almost feel the gravel gritting in his throat as he said: "Folks, these are the blues. From way down home. In the south-land of Brooklyn. They tell a story of sweat falling from people sitting on stoops on hot summer nights. Too hot for them in bed. They ain't got no money. Got nothing but the pain of fighting a lost cause. So what can they do? They sing, yes, they sing the blues ..."

"Shit," Little Jimmie said.

"Let's have another joint," I said, "and get this show on the road."

"Yeah. We gotta see the man," Little Jimmie put in.

"The man?" The Duke asked, frowning.

"Yes," I said. "The A & R man at Paradise records."

SEVEN

After clansmen goodbyes, we were mellow. I wanna tell you: every muscle and vein in our bodies relaxed. We moved out on to the Avenue like crack athletes, briefly spotlighted by the fickle March sun. The Avenue was deserted and quiet except for the long-drawn-out cries of a hungry child. A rare cry. Normally, the Avenue's children were well fed, healthy, and happy.

"Terrible. Ain't it?" I said, looking up and down the Avenue.

A wave of old-star glory had washed over Little Jimmie. "It'll all be over soon. Remember when I was a star? Butter and biscuits and Smithfield ham every day. I was one of the big wheels in the machine. It'll be like the old days after we cut our first side."

"We can't miss," I said. "We've got too much going for us."

In an extravagant mood, I hailed a taxi, a sinister yellow taxi, festooned with leather straps and Bessemer steel rods. What looked like black blood caked the rear fender. The driver was a small pale man with an open face.

"Good morning," he said in a quavery voice. "I am at your service."

"Paradise," I snarled, easing into the taxi.

"That's Broadway and Fifty-second Street," Little Jimmie said.

"The musical capital of the world. We're part of the action."

"You're very fortunate," the pale taxi driver said.

Little Jimmie and I exchanged blasé-celebrity glances and laughed.

"Did I say something wrong?" the driver asked.

"Wrong," Little Jimmie exclaimed. "Listen to this turd."

Sweat showed on the driver's face. "Yes, sir. That's what I am. A turd. But you people are the greatest. You have so much soul. And how you can sing and dance. You must be the happiest people on the face of the earth."

"Cut the lip," I said. "Get this show on the road."

The perspiring driver swallowed hard and replied softly, "Yes, sir."

The sinister taxi started off smoothly enough and went down Fifth Avenue, leaving the upper Avenue's strong odor of decay. The denuded trees of Central Park formed a bleak bower, and, on the opposite side, glass fronts of apartment buildings gleamed. It was as if the architects had all worked from a single design.

Now the taxi was at Eighty-second and Fifth. Little Jimmie dozed. I watched the parkside where gouty, snobbish mongrel dogs howled discontentedly. Infected infants sat in Rolls-Royce baby carriages guarded by gaunt nursemaids. Good Humor men equipped with transistor laugh-

ing machines hawked extrasensory and paranoiac ice-
cream bars. The unemployed formed a sad sea in front of
the apartment buildings: they jostled, spat, bit, and hit
each other in the stomach, their voices a medley of frustrated cries, while merry apartment wives peered from
plate-glass windows, hiding smiles behind Fascisti silk
fans.

The pot was surely working, I thought hazily.

I closed my eyes and saw my Deb behind her own
plate-glass window, spoon-feeding Lester Jefferson II—
Little Les, while, twenty floors below, I polished the Mer-
cedes with Mr. Clean. It could happen: rebirth in this land,
or was such a birth only an exit from the womb, not a door
to the future?

Life is one pot dream after another, I thought, and,
yawning, I turned to Little Jimmie. "We're on our way," I
said.

"It's in the bag."

Suddenly the driver's chattering teeth caught our ears.

"What's wrong with him?" Little Jimmie asked.

"Guess he's got thin blood."

"He's a skinny little son of a bitch."

"It's a wonder the wind doesn't blow his ass away."

Little Jimmie chuckled, and leaned back in the seat like
a king.

"I ain't cold," the pleasant-faced driver cried. "I'm
scared to death. I know you gonna take my leather straps

and chains and beat me up. I know you gonna make black-
and-blue marks all over me and take my money. Ain't that
right? Ain't that right?"

Sighing, Little Jimmie said, "Is he trying to get in on the
act?"

"No, man. He's a masochist. Dig?"

"Come on," the driver shouted. "Beat me and get it over
with. I can't stand the waiting."

"Don't blow your cool," I warned him.

"Ain't that right, ain't that right?" Little Jimmie laughed.

"Sounds like the title of our second solid-gold-hit
record."

Just then the taxi driver picked up speed, raced down
Fifth Avenue to Sixty-second Street, where he slammed on
the brakes.

"All right," he sneered. "Shut your trap. I've had enough
from you jokers."

"Dig this mother," I said.

"What was that?" the driver snapped.

"Lay off, man," Little Jimmie said.

The taxi zoomed through a blinking red light and came
to the fountain fronting the Plaza.

"Boys," the pale taxi driver began clearly, "you ain't on
home ground now. You had your chance. So now don't
you blow your cool. This is my turf. We're *downtown.*"

"I know, I know," I sighed.

"Yeah," Little Jimmie put in, "but we're the two new

BB's from Tin Pan Alley. You wouldn't wanna do nothing that would fuck up the economy and cause an international incident, would you?"

"Jesus," the taxi driver exclaimed. "Wait until I tell the kids and my old lady. Jesus. You could have had a police escort all the way downtown. Get you away from the Harlem riffraff. I knew all along that you two gentlemen were something special. The riffraff is causing all the trouble. Making it bad for you colored people."

"I know, I know," I sighed again as we swung on to Central Park South. I ran a moist hand through The Wig. It was still soft, luxurious, and together. Visions of fame and fortune bounced through the soul of The Wig: The Deb, the girl next door, the girl at the end of the double rainbow.

We turned on to Broadway. The driver said, "Oh, the way you boys can sing!" He paused, breathing hard. "Never knew a colored person that didn't have a fine singing voice."

Crossing Broadway and Fifty-seventh Street, I was a one-man chorus. "I know, I know," I sang.

"You're the greatest, you're the tops," the pale driver said.

"Oh yes, oh yes," I sang.

Straight-faced, Little Jimmie Wishbone looked out the window.

"Now don't get me wrong," the driver chuckled pleasantly, slowing at Broadway and Fifty-second Street. "That'll be three-fifty even."

Like a late winter grasshopper, he jumped out and opened the rear door. "It's been a real pleasure and I wish you guys the best."

I got out of the sinister yellow taxi slowly, like an old man who knows his days are numbered. I did not look at the driver. I felt tired.

But Little Jimmie smiled warmly and said bitterly: "Keep the change." There was a ring of authority in his voice.

Paradise Records, Ltd., is located on the eighty-eighth floor of The League of Nations Pill Building. It straddles Broadway and Fifty-second Street like a chipped marble pyramid and is topped by a cone-shaped tower sporting five revolving neon crosses. Piped music echoes from the lobby to the tower: opera, symphonies, sweet ballads, American rock 'n' roll, and selected international hits.

We stepped smartly through the lobby to the strains of "Nearer My God to Thee," the number-one song on the nuclear hit parade.

"Next week it'll be us," I said, breaking into a wild grin.

"It's in the bag," Little Jimmie said brightly. Only eighty-eight floors and a new career. He'd recapture his public image. I watched him square the felt hat, flip the brim down over his left eye. There was even a glint of ex-pectation in that eye.

"Gotta rent me a Caddie," he said. "Can't be seen making it through the streets in a taxi. My fans wouldn't like that."

I pressed the elevator button. "How do you feel?"

"Like being born again. I know how you feel too, on the first wave of fame."

The wide doors of the elevator swung outward like the doors of a saloon. Little Jimmie braced sloping shoulders and pushed past me.

"Let's go, boy," he said.

A sudden thought hit me. "We don't have a manager," I said.

"It doesn't matter at this stage of the game. Press the button. Eighty-eight. I'll do the talking. You know I'm an old hand at this type of thing. But in the past, people always came to me. Either to my Beverly Hills mansion or to my Manhattan penthouse. But we'll manage."

The elevator closed silently. We stood stiff and proud, our hot eyes focused on the walls of the elevator. The walls were eye-catching: mahogany, with carved musical scales and American-dollar signs.

"Lucre, my ghost," Little Jimmie sighed.

"You're a swinging stud."

"Nothing to it, boy. I know what's happening. I've had too many gigs."

Exiting from the elevator, I prayed for ten thousand one-night stands, for a million six-week holdovers. Balloon images of The Deb burst inside my excited beautiful head. I was happy like a man when a particularly painful wound begins to heal. I was no longer jockeying for position: I was in position. I followed Little Jimmie through the great bronze doors of Paradise Records.

The receptionist was licking stamps, and a sequined sign on the desk said: Miss Belladonna.

"Yes?" Miss Belladonna said in a hoarse voice, without looking up.

"We're the two new BB's and we want a hearing," Little Jimmie said with great dignity.

"Yeah?"

"Yes, young lady."

Miss Belladonna yawned. "Well ..."

Impatient, Little Jimmie drummed his fingers on the kidney-shaped glass desk.

"Look alive, young lady," he warned sternly.

Giggling, Miss Belladonna said, "I'm sorry. You know how things are in Paradise. All this *joie de vivre* jazz. We're ever so busy, too. One hit after another."

"I know," I said, "but we're gonna make an explosion in Paradise."

Miss Belladonna showed us her jaundiced eyes. Lips trembling, she pressed a gold button and seized a hand mike.

"Mr. Pingouin! Mr. Pingouin! Front and center," she sang.

Then, clasping hands over a flat chest, she cried: "Oh! This is so thrilling. I've seen the best of them walk through that door. Just walk right in and open their mouth and—*cling-a-ling-a-ling*—the coins literally roll off their tongues, and it's so thrilling!"

Little Jimmie beamed. "That's the way it goes. But you gotta have star quality."

"Yes," I said quickly. "Stars are always collected and cool." It was something I had read in a gossip column. I liked the sound: collected and cool.

"Cool?" Mr. Pingouin purred, minueting into the reception room.

A young man, dapper in banker's gray and wearing large, round, fashionable glasses. He looked like a happy Uncle Bunny Owl.

"Welcome to Paradise. The home of hits."

"Naturally, I am aware," the comeback star hee-hawed. "I is Little Jimmie Wishbone from Auk-in-saw."

"Little Jimmie Wishbone from Arkansas?" Mr. Pingouin asked, his round glasses skiing down his smooth nose.

"Little Jimmie Wishbone," Miss Belladonna gasped.

"The late-late show and the afternoon soap opera? My mother just loved *Southern Sunset.* She's seen it seven times."

"And no residuals," Little Jimmie added painfully.

"Forget it," Mr. Pingouin said with a wave of the hand. "I know you are money."

"Oh! It's so thrilling," Miss Belladonna cooed. "Shall I call Mr. Sunflower Ashley-Smithe?"

"Mr. Ashley-Smithe is our A & R man," Mr. Pingouin informed us.

"What about promotion?" Little Jimmie wanted to know.

"We have the networks and the press by the balls," Mr. Pingouin said, smiling shyly.

"I should say we have," Miss Belladonna said. She seized the hand mike. "Mr. Sunflower Ashley-Smithe. Front and center!"

Silence, a rich soft silence, enfolded the nonchalant future recording stars, the jaundiced receptionist, and the owl-eyed first assistant vice-president.

Presently, doleful Muzak came on with Napoleon's Funeral March. Little Jimmie stood at attention, Miss Belladonna seemed to doze, Mr. Pingouin bowed his head, and I counted to one hundred.

Then Mr. Sunflower Ashley-Smithe entered to the strains of "Home on the Range."

There was nothing unusual about Mr. Sunflower Ashley-Smithe. A thoroughbred American Negro, the color of bittersweet chocolate—chocolate that looked as if it had weathered many seasons of dust, rain, and darkness, chocolate that had not been eaten, but simply left to dehydrate. He was more than six feet tall, I guessed. And when he smiled at us, I knew my ship was docking at last.

"Gentlemen," he said, and bowed sedately. "I know ours will be a perfect relationship. Now, will you please join me in the inner room."

"It's our pleasure," Little Jimmie bowed back.

"Oh! Goodness," Miss Belladonna squealed. "This is so exciting. It always is."

"Have a happy session," Mr. Pingouin said, "and please remember that you are in the hands of Paradise."

Despite an abundance of expensive flowering plants, the inner room had the serene masculinity of a GI sleeping bag. Facing the window wall were two baby-grand pianos with smooth brass finishes. Large lounge chairs formed a fat lime green circle centered on a stainless-steel coffee table. It was a large pleasant room, ideal for music.

"Gentlemen," Mr. Sunflower Ashley-Smithe said, extending the pale pink palm of his dark hand, "please be seated. Everything is very informal here at Paradise. That is the key to our worldwide success."

Finger popping, Little Jimmie agreed. "That's the method. When I was making my last trilogy of flicks about homesteaders ... Wow! Remember? Everyone went ape over them. Took the Cannes, Venice, and Berlin film festivals by storm. Well, *my* method was always to have a relaxed set. Even on location."

"You were one of my heroes, Mr. Wishbone. Pity you couldn't bridge the changeover. Perhaps your new career will rectify the situation."

"Mr. Ashley-Smithe, you are a knight of humanity. The first star—the first *flower,* of deep emotions. The musical genius of this century."

"You're very kind, sir."

Lord, this was getting too much. Trembling, I broke in: "We're relaxed and ready to sing, Mr. Sunflower Ashley-Smithe."

"Fine, fine," the first flower of deep emotions said, rubbing his hands and executing a nimble ballet turn.

No music penetrated the cork-lined inner room. There was only a brush-fire silence until the graceful A *&* R man faced us.

"It's so soft … easy," he said. "Two groovy-colored studs. You've got everything in your favor. I know the countdown of this racket. I've worked hard to help my colored brethren and fortunately you've got what the white people want. What the *world* wants! I don't have a social life, nor do I indulge in sex. At night I go home and plot the future of my golden-voiced colored brethren. I keep a dozen milk bottles filled with lice so I won't be lonely. I never have a dull or idle moment with my happy family around me. And come morning, I'm ready to face this mother-grabbing racket again. Understand?"

"Certainly, Sunflower," Little Jimmie said.

"Certainly, Mr. Ashley-Smithe," I said.

"Fine, fine. Now please join me at the baby."

Riffling through the plastic attaché case, Little Jimmie

said, "Let's run through 'Harlem Nights.' It has a simple gaiety. But keep the tempo down. We have to build on this one. Know what I mean, Sunflower?"

"Oh yes. Exactly."

Little Jimmie strode manfully over to the baby-grand piano. "Let's take it from the top, Les."

"Yeah, baby. Let's go. I'm in excellent voice this morning."

Bowing again, Mr. Sunflower Ashley-Smithe rippled the keyboard expertly. "Wonderful. Your choice of an opener is great."

Little Jimmie cleared his throat and peered at the sheet music closely. "Now, I'll take the verse and you take the chorus, Les. Let's rip a gut. This must be spontaneous."

The musical genius of the century laughed vigorously. "Let's see if you're colored."

Camaraderie like sunlight filled the inner room. I really felt as if I *could* bust a gut. I wasn't embarking on a Madison Avenue or a Wall Street career. No, this gig was glamour, Broadway, night lights. Champagne supper clubs, call girls, paying off bellboys and the police. A million hysterical teenagers screaming, clamoring for your auto-graph, a strand of your curly hair, a snotty Kleenex, a toothpick, a bad cavity filling, a pawnshop diamond ring, and all because few parents are child-oriented. And now *I* was a part of the racket!

"Lester," Little Jimmie said sharply.

"I'm with you, baby."

"Ready?" Mr. Ashley-Smith asked.

I watched Little Jimmie flex his muscles, clench his fist, and breathe deeply. So deep I could see the outline of his soul on his sweating face.

And then he began to sing as if he were alone in a splendid garden on a cool summer morning. Looking at his contorted face, I thought: what a magnificent actor. A Harlem-born great actor.

Mr. Ashley-Smithe was impressed too. He clasped his hands and closed his eyes.

"The rebirth of my hero," he whispered.

Gesturing, alone in the garden, Little Jimmie's voice filled the inner room.

> *Harlem nights are gloomy and long*
> *A cold, cold landscape*
> *Darkness, darkness.*
> *Will I ever lift up my voice ...*
> *And sing,* I falsettoed right on key.

"You curly headed son of a bitch," Little Jimmie yelled, "you didn't bust a gut!"

"What?" I faltered.

The first flower of deep emotions moaned. "My brothers, my fellow countrymen. Please. Please, stop. Let's take a break."

The comeback lion was fuming. "Yes. Let's take a *long* break!"

Hurt, I silently vowed to go it on my own. Solo, baby. Who needed a washed-up movie star!

When I came out of my sulky reverie, I heard Mr. Ashley-Smithe's voice: "I work very hard, I am a good man. I do not practice black magic. I love my fellow man and that includes white people ..." Mr. Ashley-Smithe paused. "So how could this happen to me?"

What was the mother-grabber talking about? I couldn't make it out, though Little Jimmie seemed to know. He looked like a freshly cast mummy. Hump him! I'd go it alone.

"I could try 'Limehouse Blues,' Mr. Sunflower," I enunciated clearly. "I think I could fake a Chinese accent. 'Limehouse Blues' is a particular favorite of mine, and an all-time classic, as you well know."

Mr. Sunflower Ashley-Smithe seemed to be trying to check a bathtub of tears. "That won't be necessary," he said. "Would you gentlemen kindly leave? Both of you. You are both a disgrace to your colored brethren *and* to this great republic! Why, you poor slobs can't even carry a tune."

The first flower of human emotions arose from the piano. His laughter was loud and frightening.

EIGHT

No laughter welded my shocked dark heart. I marched swiftly out of the inner room, past Miss Belladonna, who seeing my face screamed, "Goodness!"

Waiting impatiently for the elevator, I wanted to scream myself. The Wayward Four rocked, rolled, wallowed through the loudspeaker Muzak. *"Play-a simple melody, play-a simple melody,"* they sang. Off-key, no doubt spitting their puberty juice. "A racket," Sunflower Ashley-Smithe had said. Well, I wanted no part of it. Right then and there, I told myself, it had been an impulsive, foolish mistake. I was destined for a higher calling. Perhaps not Madison Avenue or Wall Street. No. A real man-sized job. A porter, a bus boy, a shoeshine boy, a swing on my father's old Pullman run. Young Abe by the twenty-watt bulb. Sweating, toiling, studying the map of The Great Society. One is not defeated until one is defeated. Hadn't the drugstore prophet said, "You may become whatever you desire?" Perhaps I'd even become a politician or a preacher—those wingless guards against tyranny and misery.

The saloon doors of the elevator opened. Piously, I entered. Muzak thundered with a gospel group singing:

This little Light of mine . . .
I'm gonna let it shine . . .

I ran my hand through The Wig and stamped my feet
until the elevator reached the ground floor.

The lobby was teeming with the fabulous show-biz
crowd, yak-yaking, hustling. Well, they could yak and hus-
tle without me.

I decided, however, to wait for Little Jimmie. My anger
had cooled and I wanted to talk with him quietly. Plus, I
didn't want those earnest boys from Kings County to nab
him on Broadway. I waited for what seemed a long time
and then I spied him standing against a piece of blowtorch
sculpture, looking like a confident young executive with
big deals brewing.

"You were up there a long time. What happened?"

Little Jimmie hee-hawed. "Oh, you know how it is, Les.
Show-biz talk. Putting out feelers. Sunflower said he
thought we were too tense. Nerves."

"Is that what he said?"

"Yeah. Told him I'd meet him tonight. He suggested the
Copa. But I said Jilly's. More intimate."

"That's great," I said.

"It's boss, man," Little Jimmie smiled.

And we didn't say another word until we emerged from
the League of Nations Pill Building, blinking at the ferocious midday sun.

"Think we could go to Europe and gain some experience?" I asked.

"It's an idea," Little Jimmie said gravely. "I ain't been in Europe in a long time. They know me over there."

"Let's go for coffee," I suggested.

"No, Les."

"Then let's go some place. What about digging those Harlem society broads?"

"I don't wanna see no society chicks." Little Jimmie started walking off, walking up Fifty-second Street.

"Where you going?"

"I don't know. Just going."

"See you later," I said.

"Yeah. Later."

I watched my slow-shuffling friend disappear into the noonday crowd. The mambo strains of "Happy Days Are Here Again" drifted from a nearby record shop.

NINE

The sun was very bright the following morning; there was something almost nice about the polluted air. I had my glass of lukewarm tap water, said my Christian prayers, recited a personal Koran, and kissed the rat-gnawed floorboards of my room. (Nonbelievers, please take note: I was definitely insane, an ambitious lunatic.) I had spent a sleepless night plotting and thinking. Impersonation is an act of courage, as well as an act of skill, for the impersonator must be cold-hearted, aware of his limitations. I, however, suddenly realized I *had* no limitations. I felt good. The sun was shining. Bathed in its warm rays, I became Apollo's Saturday morning son. My new image had crystallized. An aristocratic image, I might add. The new image was based on The Wig, and was to be implemented by the forethought of Mr. Fishback. It took me a little while to accept the fact that I was going to act upon it, but I did.

Here is the timetable: 10 A.M., perspiring. 10:15, borrowed two cigarettes from Nonnie Swift. Three minutes of cheers; Nonnie had been barred from the Harlem Sewing Circle because of her Creole past. Quarter of eleven, a last status sip of lukewarm water. At two minutes to eleven I snatched Mr. Fishback's Christmas gift from under the sofa bed: an all-purpose, fake, forged credit card, guaranteed at five hundred hospitals in all fifty states. Honored instantly by one thousand fine hotels and restaurants, plus major service stations, and airlines. Car-rental agencies also guaranteed. With Mr. Fishback's dandy all-purpose card, I was going into orbit.

As a result, I found myself at 1 P.M. alighting from a chauffeur-driven Silver Cloud Rolls-Royce on Sutton Place South. In my Fourteenth Street–Saville Row suit (dark, synthetic, elegant) that I'd bought from Mr. Fishback—I was truly *together*. And the six joints of Haitian marijuana I'd smoked on the way down made me feel powerful. Like Cassius Clay. Like Hitler. Like Fats Domino. Like Dick Tracy. I dismissed the car and driver. They'd done their work, I had my high, and I saw no reason to push my luck.

I walked through Ionic columns and on to the plastic-marblite-tiled courtyard of the Riverview Tower Apartment Residence (the last stronghold of concentrated capitalists) to receive a sharp clicking of heels from the amazed doorman.

"*Bon jour,* Mac," I said, between clenched teeth.

The doorman saluted smartly. "Good afternoon, sir," he said clearly, opening the entrance door. "Lovely weather for March, isn't it, sir?"

"Smashing," I replied, scanning dark clouds. "Is the lift self-service?"

"Yes, sir."

"Pity."

"Yes, sir."

"The modern world is going to hell."

"Quite right, sir. Would you like me to press the elevator button? They were made in Japan. Amazing little gadgets, and I'd be honored if you'd grant me permission to push the button for you."

"Oh, yes. By all means. Jolly good of you."

There were tears in the doorman's eyes. "Thank you, sir."

"What's your name, old chap?"

"Abraham O'Reilly, sir."

"O'Reilly. A fine name. Must remember that."

"God bless you, sir."

Joyfully, I waltzed into the elevator and ascended upward, heavenward.

The elevator did not quite reach the ramparts of heaven. It stopped on the ninetieth floor, the penthouse floor.

I got out and felt my feet plowing into a deep shaggy Greek carpet, a sensation not altogether pleasant, but I was determined to maintain my bored-rich-boy expression. I pressed a well-scrubbed finger against the doorbell and waited.

Tom Lacy opened the penthouse door. Tomming a wee bit, he bowed and rolled his eyes. He seemed not to recognize me. Was The Wig that effective?

"Ain't nobody home. They is in the country," he said. "Won't be back till late Monday morning."

"You're the man I wanna see."

Moaning, Tom Lacy looked away. "Mister, I ain't done nothing and I ain't buying nothing. Good day."

"Just one moment, please."

"Mister," Tom whined, "I done told you already. I ain't buying nothing. I gits plenty of good used clothing from the boss, and the mistress throws a few hand-me-downs to the old lady. I got plenty of insurance and a wristwatch that runs jest fine. I'm scared of cars. And as you can see, skin lightener will do me no good and I'm dead set against hair grease and don't try to sell me no back lot in Westchester, cause I ain't buying. But come back Monday. They'll be back then."

Yesterday at Paradise Records, Ltd., in a moment of panic, I tried like hell to bust a gut. Now, staring hard at Tom Lacy, staring at his sweaty immobile face, I tried not to bust a gut.

Slightly envious of his brilliant impersonation, I said, "Shit."

"Mister. I didn't mean to offend you. I jest don't need nothing. I is way up to my ears in debt already."

"Okay, Tom. Can the cat. It's me. Your boy Les. Ask me in and fix a drink."

Tom Lacy stared hard at me. Gritting his alabaster-coated false teeth, he let the placid mask of his face change to that of a natural killer.

Just to be on the safe side, I took several steps backward.

"I ain't in the mood for no jokes. I had to work my ass off to get them bastards to the country."

"Man, you just ain't with the happenings. You're non-progressive."

"Youyouyou ..." Tom Lacy shouted.

"Control yourself," I said. "You're sweating too hard and might catch a cold."

His eyes zeroed in on my Wig. Before I could open my mouth, he lunged like a besotted bull, rammed his kinky head into my stomach, and knocked me flat on my back.

"Tom!"

"A little louder."

"TOM!"

"That's more like it. Now, do you have any last-minute special requests?"

"Yes. Get your mother-grabbing hands from around my neck. I can hardly breathe."

"I only asked for last-minute requests, and I'm doing you a favor at that. You were once my friend."

Tom weighed only 170 pounds but his grip was force-
ful. I could hardly breathe. His hands played a teasing,
sadistic game on my neck.

"Tom, old buddy ..."

"I don't wanna hear that jazz."

"Tom, please. I'm flat on my back. Let me up and I'll explain."

He groaned. I could see tears mixing with the sweat.
His Adam's apple went up and down like a yo-yo.

"What's wrong with you?" he shouted.

"Nothing. Tom ..."

"Have you gone crazy? This ain't Halloween."

"Please take your hands off my neck," I said, struggling
for breath.

"You've lost your mind," Tom Lacy sobbed.

"I haven't lost my mind. Now will you please let me up?
I'm getting full of goat's hair."

He bit his lower lip and let go. "Les, you've taken ten
years off my life ..."

Sobbing immodestly, he rose slowly. I felt like a jackass.

"I never thought you'd do something like this," Tom
said.

"Do what?" I asked angrily. I got up and ran a cautious
hand through The Wig. "You must be off your rocker."

"I've known you a long time, Les. I've known you since
you were born. I was your godfather. I know you were or-

phaned at an early age and that your life has been nothing but trials and tribulations ..."

"Tom, what are you getting at?"

"Shut up," my grieving friend commanded. "Don't interrupt. I'm trying to talk to you like a father. Yes, trials and tribulations. You were such a good boy. Your dear parents taught you to read and write. You had good manners and went to Sunday School. And you've got a sturdy head on your shoulders. I was always proud when I never found your name on the sports page of the *Daily News* listed among them juvenile delinquents."

"Tom. You're breaking my goddam heart."

"WHAT HAVE YOU DONE TO YOUR BEAUTIFUL HAIR?"

"Nothing," I said.

"Infidel!" Tom Lacy accused in a shaking voice and lunged at me again.

I jumped back quickly. "Listen to me. Please. I'm doing this for the sit-ins. Did you hear me? I'm doing this for the sit-ins."

"The sit-ins?" Tom Lacy's dawning smile was absolutely saintly. "Great day in the morning!"

"Yeah," I grinned. "What a morning."

"Man, you had me scared to death," Tom said.

"I was a little uneasy myself."

Tom wiped his sweaty brow. "What would the hero like to drink? Champagne? A little Château Haut-Brion?

Or could he whip me up a quick snack? Rossini steak? Creamed eggs in ramekins, slightly gratiné, floating in caviar?"

"No. Double vodka on the rocks. Gotta work a picket line this afternoon."

"Okay, sport," Tom smiled. "I *knew* you'd never betray us!"

Settling back in a down-stuffed chair, I said, "How could I possibly betray you?"

"Your parents would be proud of you."

"How's the chart coming along?"

Tom frowned sadly. "Not too good, Les. According to this morning's *Times,* only 117 died."

"That isn't too bad," I said, accepting the vodka.

"There have been better days," Tom said, pulling up a comfortable chair, a kind of Chinese rocking chair.

"Of course," I agreed. "Still, you can't complain. Anyway, Easter is coming, and after that it will be vacation time all over America."

"I know. But I like New Year's Eve better."

"I heard on the radio this morning that a jet crashed and killed forty-five."

"Really?" Tom exclaimed. "That's wonderful. That tops the fire at the old-folks' home in Jersey. Only nine of them burned."

"A woman was strangled in Philly yesterday."

"Usually there are more sex murders in the spring."

"That's true," I agreed.

Tom was very excited. "Let's toast to spring."

"To spring and to death," I said, raising my vodka glass.

"That's a great toast. Sure you don't want me to open a magnum of champagne? Thirty-four. A good year."

"No. I'll stick to vodka. Don't forget, I'll be out in the cold, picketing until sundown."

"You are a fine young man," Tom said quietly. "I'm proud of you."

"You're an earthly angel."

"You're Moses walking in the wilderness!" Tom said jumping up suddenly. The Waterford chandelier prisms tinkled merrily.

"To spring and to death," Tom announced rapturously. "We're making progress, Les. In fifty years there won't *be* any white people!"

"There'll always be white people," I told him.

Tom Lacy was a stunned Negro man. He seemed to age again. "You really think so?"

"Yes, Tom. They'll be having babies, you know."

"I always keep forgetting that," Tom said.

"But they'll be a minority by then," I assured him.

"Oh, that'll be the day," Tom Lacy cried. "I come from a long line of human beings, too. My people was Watusi. Cattle barons. I'm seven feet tall in my stocking feet, as you well know. Your folks never talked much about family background. Do you know where your folks came from?"

I polished off my drink and shook my head. "I don't

know exactly. I don't know much about my family tree. Although I've heard we're descended from the Queen of Sheba, Marco Polo, and Pope Paul the Fifth."

"That's mighty impressive. Funny I never heard your ma and pa mention that, or any of your other relatives."

"We're very modest."

"If I were you, I wouldn't worry," Tom told me. "Family trees don't mean much these days."

"I'm sure happy to hear that."

Rocking, Tom looked as warm and shrewd as Harry Golden. "Yes. We're making progress. Finally things are looking up."

"You're right," I said. "Now the Puerto Ricans are getting shit from the fan."

Tom Lacy had a faraway look in his eyes, and they were misty. "No. It won't be long now."

A tugboat droned on the East River. I don't know why, but I suddenly thought of Abe Lincoln, and Thomas Jefferson too, and all the people who had made me believe in them. I leaned forward in my chair, dead serious, and listened to my godfather's wisdom.

My godfather shook his weary head. "Lord. I can hardly wait to act like a natural man. I've had to Tom so much that it's hard for me to knock it off. I even shuffle and keep my eyes on the floor when I'm talking to my own wife."

"I know what you mean. When I'm in a restaurant and leave a tip, I feel as if I'd committed a sin."

"That's a fact," Tom agreed. "It's like giving myself a tip somehow."

"By the way, godfather. Could you let me hold fifty?"

"What?"

"Fifty dollars."

"I ain't got no money," my godfather whined. "It takes every cent I get for those charts. I have to subscribe to every daily and weekly newspaper in the country."

"Have I ever failed to come through? Who went downtown with his little red wagon and got all those old newspapers when you were in bed with the flu last winter?"

"What you need it for?"

"Haven't I got to eat in all those segregated restaurants?"

"You're right," Tom Lacy agreed, reaching for his wallet. "Are you sure fifty will be enough?"

Strutting down Sutton, I perhaps looked like a happy citizen of Manhattan but my real roots were deep in the countryside that had produced people like my dead parents and, yes, Tom Lacy. One day, one fine day, Tom and Aunt Bessie would be proud of me.

"I'll shake up this town if it's the last thing I do," I vowed to the sky, serene and gray, watching a train of pigeons wing down on the balcony of an apartment building. Their drippings looked like some rare melting metal.

The wind was receding. I walked over to the parklike promenade of Sutton Place South. Freshly planted trees (each tree discreetly sporting a name tag) lined the promenade. I glanced at the expensive trees and then looked down at the sewer waters of the East River.

Lester Jefferson was at peace with himself.

Hadn't I been trying since day before yesterday? Goodness. Plotting and thinking, plotting and thinking. And hadn't every happening bounced right back in my face? Ding-dong-doom.

There had been one moment: The Deb. She had made me feel warm, alive, ambitious. She had taken a piece of my heart without knowing it. With the crisp fifty neatly stashed in my jacket pocket, I knew what I wanted most was to see her.

"Mister," I heard a voice behind me call.

I turned and saw an apathetic-looking middle-aged Negro, a man.

"Could you spare a cigarette, Mister?"

"What are you doing over here?" I said severely. "Don't you know beggars aren't allowed over here?"

"I ain't no beggar," the man said. "I'm a runaway slave."

"Don't give me that shit. You half-assed con man. Slavery was outlawed years ago. Centuries ago."

"You're wrong," the man said in a quiet voice. He unbuttoned his tattered trousers. "Look at this if you don't believe me."

Around the man's waist was a flexible chastity belt at

least ten inches wide. Engraved letters on the belt read: "I paid good money for this sturdy black man. He belongs to me and not to God."

"No," I screamed and started running.

"Wait," the slave cried.

Frightened, I halted at the promenade's entrance, marked by a bronze plaque:

LIFE IS WORTHWHILE,

FOR IT IS FULL OF DREAMS AND

PEACE, GENTLENESS AND ECSTASY,

AND FAITH THAT BURNS LIKE A

CLEAR WHITE FLAME ON A GRIM

DARK ALTAR.

I got the fifty from my suit-coat pocket and gave it to the man—not because I was frightened or generous or worried about sleepless nights—I gave the man the fifty because he *looked* like a slave. I knew he was a slave. I have a genius for detecting slaves.

"Thank you and may God bless you," the slave said.

"You'd better get something to eat and a room," I said.

Then I turned off Sutton Place South and walked up Fifty-fourth Street and up First Avenue toward home, toward Harlem.

TEN

It was Saturday night. The sky was starscaped, and home-spun rib-tickling brotherly love had settled over the city. You felt it even at the frontier gate, above Ninety-sixth Street, leading to the Badlands of Harlem. The air was different too, with a strange smell rather like mildewed bread. And I, too, managed to be happy (courtesy of Mr. Fishback's Christmas gift): at the end of the evening, The Deb had come home with me.

Now while Saturday night turned into cold Sunday, I copulated like crazy. My groin ached.

"You're too much," I said.

"Whee!" The Deb somersaulted and wiggled her toes. "You've made me extremely happy, Mr. Jefferson."

"Do Debs really like that?"

The gyrating Deb moaned.

I wiped my forehead, watching The Deb's rhythmic buttocks. "Wanna be a slave, baby?"

"Yes. Come on, lover. It really moves me."

"Take it easy, little woman."

"Please. It drives me out of my gardenia-picking mind."

"I've had enough," I sighed.

"Don't you wanna make me happy?"

"Yes," I said slowly, trying to play a cool hand.

"Ain't I been good to you?"

"Yes," I admitted, feeling clammy, feeling that I was playing a losing hand.

"Then move me, sweetie," The Deb teased. "I ain't dead. I can be moved."

"No," I said firmly.

The lyrically pretty Deb pouted. "Finky-foo. I'm just beginning to enjoy myself and you treat me like this. I can't help it 'cause I got kinky hair."

"Your hair has nothing to do with it."

"Yes, it does," The Deb cried. "You foreigners're always hot after us colored girls and then you throw shit into the game. Why don't you go to Africa and get the real thing? And as far as I'm concerned you can take your fine fine self right back across the sea."

For one quick, insane moment, I cursed the miracle sitting on top of my King James–shaped head.

The bitch. To hell with her. Tawny tiger smasher. I'd be as cool as Casanova.

Frowning, I jabbed a cigarette into the corner of my sensual thick lips.

"It's all the same to me, cupcake."

Stretching languidly, The Deb said, "Why do you treat me like this? I know you're kind and gentle. I can tell by your eyes. You look like one of those saint types I read about in grade school."

Clever, a cornucopia of cleverness. Supple, sweet. A young luxurious mountain.

I stalked over to the sofa bed. "Kiss me, baby," I said, the cigarette dangling out of the corners of my mouth.

"No."

"Broads," I spat.

"I'm like any girl. I like to be pleased."

I wanted to cry out against my own helplessness. "But, baby," I tried to explain, "didn't I show you a good time? Weren't you pampered all through dinner by the plus-ultra service way up on the sixty-fifth floor of the glittery Rainbow Room? And what about the fizzy discothèque ... where we were mobbed by all those frug people who thought we were Egyptians, and later we breezed uptown in a Duesenberg from Buckingham livery. Jesus, woman."

"That's all very true," The Deb said, "but you didn't give me any money to get my hair fixed."

"Tomorrow, love. You'd only get it messed up in bed."

"You don't want me to have my hair fixed," The Deb protested.

"That's no way to talk. Tomorrow, love. Tomorrow I'll see personally that you get the works at Helena Rubinstein."

The Deb sulked. Her body was rigid on the sofa bed. "You foreigners are just like white people. You don't like to see Negroes with good hair. You're not just satisfied with getting your rocks off ... you like to get an extra kick. By running your hand through kinky hair!"

"You don't understand," I said weakly.

"Oh, but I do! I got your number, sweetcakes."

"But you've got such wonderful hair. So natural. You want to be different, don't you?"

"I am different," The Deb informed me.

"Not if you have curly hair like me."

The Deb looked hard at me. "When I get my hair fixed tomorrow I will be like you. Almost, anyway. And pretty soon us colored people will be as white as Americans. They gonna make some pills that will turn you white over-night. Won't that be a bitch? *Everybody* will be up shit's creek then."

"You'll take all the excitement and drama out of being Negro," I laughed.

"Have you ever wanted to be a Negro? I'm not talking about daydreaming of being a Negro. I mean, have you re-ally considered it?"

"No. I'm afraid not."

"Then why have you got that suntan?" The Deb asked.

"I suppose for the same reason that you want curly hair."

"According to the Bill of Rights, which I read in grade school, being black is a sin in this country. But I never heard of curly hair being a sin."

"You're right," I said. "Now come on and give daddy a kiss."

"You know what you can do for me."

"Are you gonna be discriminating, after all I've done for you?"

"I hadn't thought of that. I simply said no."

"You're a strange girl."

"You're pretty funny yourself," The Deb glared.

Feeling an acute sense of shame, I knelt reverently beside the sofa bed. "I'm sorry, love."

"You don't love me," The Deb pouted.

"Why do you wanna act this way?"

"You know why."

"Does that really move you?"

The Deb grazed a smooth, fine brown leg against my cheek. "Pretty please."

I thought I'd die. Racked with desire, I burned my head against the side of the sofa bed.

Lightly, with the most feminine of touches, The Deb caressed The Wig.

I stiffened. Buckets of anger clogged my blood. A rebellious rage engulfed me.

"If you touch my head ..." I warned.

"Well. I do declare. If that's the way you feel."

"I'm sorry," I cried, biting my tongue, giving my hot hands orders to patrol The Deb's body.

Her flesh was warm. "Delicious," my hands radioed to my brain, and then returned to their reconnaissance patrol.

"I'll do anything for you, cupcake."

"Then do it."

I stood up. "You like it, don't you?"

"It sends me clear out of this world."

"You're just like a junkie," I teased. "Ordinary please doesn't move you."

I looked down at The Deb's face warped with pain. She closed her eyes and moaned. "Stop it! Stop torturing me. I can't stand it. Play the goddam record."

I went quickly over to the record player and put on "Rocking With It."

"Oh. You're so good to me. Come here, lover. I wanna give you the kiss-kiss of the year."

But I had to make a quick run to the bathroom, and when I returned, "Rocking With It" was almost over.

I went straight to the sofa bed. Driven by passion such as I had never known, I tried to ram my tongue down The Deb's throat.

She squirmed under my power and I understood the lust of the conquistadors.

"Daddy," she begged, "turn on the other side of 'Rocking With It.'"

"In a minute, cupcake."

"I'm gonna scream!"

"Scream," I laughed. "Scream your fucking head off. I've got you covered."

ELEVEN

Morning came as I knew it would: gray with rain. Cooing pigeons and doves. The smell of bacon grease and burnt toast and powerful black Negro coffee, spiced with potents that would enable you to face The White Man come Monday morning. The sound of Mrs. Tucker's Carolina litany could be heard through the wall. A typical Sunday morning.

Grateful, I reached up and touched something unfamiliar: The Wig, silky and very much together. Then I began to doze, until I felt The Deb's lips against my neck.

"Les, honey," she yawned. "Be a good boy. Don't be a finky-foo."

"No," I mumbled. "Not the first goddam thing in the morning."

"I hate you!"

"Go back to sleep. It's early."

"Oh. You'll be sorry."

"Knock it off, cupcake."

"I hate you!"

I had to quiet the bitch. So I pinched one buttock and commanded: "Sleep or else I knock you out of bed."

"No, you won't," The Deb sneered. "I'm getting up. I'm

cutting out. 'Go back to sleep, cupcake,'" The Deb mimicked.

She was up now, prowling around the room like an early-morning hag.

"Oh, you're one labrador retriever in the bed," she said angrily. "But ask a simple favor like turning on the record player for a little good music, and ... finky-foo."

I covered my head with the sheet and presently there was no longer the lazy beat of raindrops, or the cooing of pigeons and doves.

Early morning had exploded. The Deb had "Rocking With It" on real loud.

Bolting up in bed, I shouted: "Are you satisfied?"

"Yes, thank you."

I watched her dress, each deft movement timed to the rocking music. I felt forlorn, for there is nothing worse than a lovers' quarrel on a rainy Sunday morning. I wanted to jump out of bed and hug and kiss The Deb and say: "Baby, if that's what you wanna hear, it's all right with me."

No, I'd hold out. After all, I was Bewigged and possessed a great future, that no one could deny.

"So you're cutting out," I said.

"Indeed."

Dammit! If I had had my own natural kinky hair, "my thorny crown" (a most powerful weapon, I suddenly realized), The Deb wouldn't be switching her tail around, acting so high and mighty. She would have known by the texture of my hair that I was a mean son of a bitch. I'd have made her eat dirt.

She stood in the center of the room giving me the evil eye with her legs spread apart like those butch fruit cowboys on television and tore the wrapper from a stick of chewing gum and threw it on the floor.

"I'm cutting, shithead," The Deb said. "When you get some loot, and that means money, drop around. I sorta like you, I do." And she left, giving the door a good bang.

I lay on that cold bed, twisting, turning. I wanted to go out and strangle every last one of those pigeons and doves in the name of love and then cook them for dinner. Suffering, I didn't feel romantic or noble about letting The Deb walk out on me. Why couldn't I have found a chick who was strictly a Wig lover? No, I like drama. I had to be someone else. I had such a celestial picture of being someone else, and a part of the picture was that my luck would change. But had he? No, life still seemed to have me by the balls, stuffing poison enemas up my ass.

"Oh, well, tomorrow's Monday," I said aloud to the cockroaches on the ceiling pipes.

Then, like the first trumpet of morning, piercingly alive, like the cello of death, Nonnie Swift screamed.

"No," I sighed. In a gesture of rejection, I crossed my hands over my penis.

"Help," Nonnie cried. "I mean it this time."

"That's what the would-be suicide said when he slipped accidently off the bridge," I thought happily.

"Help! Help!"

The voice was coming closer. A mad bat with a human voice was running amok in the hall.

A rattling rap on the door.

"Les!"

I felt as if the skin were peeling off my face.

"Do you want me to break the door down?" Nonnie shouted. "I know you're in there. I always thought you were a gentleman like those cotton planters who used to court me down in New Orleans. I never thought you'd let the rats eat me up!"

I wanna tell you: pins and needles pricked my body. Rising slowly to a lotus position, I felt the glow from The Wig. My Imperial lips quivered. Tremors shook my brain. Starry brain pellets finally exploded.

Rats. *Rats!* The Magic Word.

I jumped out of bed, slid into my pants, ran to the closet, and grabbed my spear gun.

Bare-chested, barefooted, I was sort of an urban Tarzan, a knight without a charger.

"Where are the rats?" I shouted, storming out the door.

"My hero," Nonnie sang. Her face set like stone. "They're in my room. Where the hell do you think they're at?"

"Lead the way, woman."

"Follow me," Nonnie said.

And I followed, hot with excitement, clutching my spear gun, ready for the kill. One hundred rat skins would make a fine fur coat for The Deb.

TWELVE

One magnificent rat, premium blue-gray, and at least twenty-five inches long, walked boldly into the center of Nonnie Swift's cluttered living room, its near-metallic claws making a kind of snaredrum beat on the parquet floor.

"I started to call the ASPCA," Nonnie whispered.

"I'll handle this mother," I said.

"Please be careful."

"Sure thing." An old proverb crossed my mind: Bravery is a luxury; avoid it at all cost. "Take the gun," I said to Nonnie.

"Oh! Les ..."

"Take it."

A terrified Nonnie reached for the spear gun. "I'm praying as fast as I can, Lester Jefferson."

"This is gonna be child's play," I said. "Hell. I thought he'd come on like a tiger," and just then, before I could get into a quarterback position, the rat bit my left big toe.

"The sneaky son of a bitch," I yelled, hopping on one foot.

"Are you wounded?" Nonnie cried.

"No. I got tough feet."

The rat moved back. He had a meek Quaker expression and the largest yellow-green eyes I've ever seen on a rat.

"He's the lily of the valley," Nonnie said, foolishly, I thought.

"Shut up," I warned and knelt down and held out my hand. "Here, rattie, rattie," I crooned. "Come here, you sweet little bastard. Let's be pals."

"Call him Rasputin. They love that," Nonnie advised.

"Rasputin, baby. Don't be shy. Let's be pals, Rasputin."

Rasputin lowered his head and inched forward slowly.

"That's a good boy, Rasputin," I said.

And the little bugger grazed my hand lovingly. Rasputin's fake chinchilla fur was warm, soft.

"That's a good little fellow," I smiled sweetly and clamped my hands so hard around Rasputin's throat that his yellow-green eyes popped out and rolled across the parquet like dice.

"Oh, my gracious," Nonnie exclaimed. "You killed him with your bare hands. Oh, my gracious!"

"It was a fair fight."

"Yes, it was, Lester Jefferson. You killed the white bastard with your hands."

"Yeah. He's a dead *gray* son of a bitch," I said happily.

"He's a dead *white* son of a bitch," Nonnie insisted. "White folks call you people coons, but never rat, 'cause that's *them.*"

"I didn't know that."

"It's a fact. I should know. They got plenty of rats in New Orleans. But none in the Garden District, where I was born."

"Well, well," I said. "You never get too old to learn." Seizing my rusty Boy Scout knife from my patched hip pocket, I began skinning Rasputin I. "Do you think the others will be afraid to come out because they smell the odor of death?" I said.

A delighted cackle from Miss Swift. She lifted her skirt and displayed rose, well-turned knees. "Let'm come. You can handle'm."

"You're right for once."

Nonnie walked over to me, like a fifty-year-old cheerleader. She touched my shoulder lightly. "Your true glory has flowered," she said. "Samson had his hair and, by god! you got your Wig."

Modesty forbade me to answer Miss Swift, but her voice rang sweetly in my ears. I would have kissed her, except my hands were soaked with blood.

"Are you ready, warrior?"

"At your service, Ma'am."

"That's the spirit," Nonnie said. "I'll get the coal shovel and bang against the wall. Then I'll close my eyes. I don't want my baby to be born with the sign of a rat on him."

Waiting for Nonnie's overture, I stood up and stretched. The blood had caked on my hands, making them itchy.

"This is gonna be more fun than a parade," Nonnie said. She spat on the coal shovel for luck.

"I'm ready when you are," I said, bracing my shoulders and sucking in my belly.

"Here we go," Nonnie cried, and banged the shovel against the wall three sharp whacks.

Lord! Eight rats bred from the best American bloodlines (and one queer little mouse) jumped from holes in the *chinoiserie* panels. Nonnie had her eyes tight shut and was humming "Reach Out for Me." Or were the rats humming? I couldn't quite tell.

Fearless, I didn't move an inch. Images of heroes marched through my Wigged head. I would hold the line. I would prove that America was still a land of heroes.

Widespread strong hands on taut hips, fuming, ready for action—I stomped my feet angrily. If I'd had a cape, I'd have waved it.

The rats advanced with ferocious cunning.

Perhaps for half a second, I trembled—slightly.

With heavy heart and nothing else, Nonnie Swift prayed. Through the thin wall, I heard Mrs. Tucker wheeze a doubtful, "Amen."

Then, suddenly feeling a more than human strength (every muscle in my body rippled), I shouted, "All right, ya dirty rats!"

My voice shook the room. Nonnie moaned, "Mercy on

us." I could hear Mrs. Tucker's harvest hands applauding on the other side of the wall. The rats had stopped humming but continued to advance.

And I went to meet them, quiet as Seconal (this was not the moment for histrionics)—it would have been foolhardy of me to croon, "Rasputin, old buddy."

Arms outstretched, the latest thing in human crosses, I tilted my chin, lifted my left leg, and paused.

They came on at a slow pace, counting time. The mouse shrewdly remained near the wastebasket, just under the lavabo.

"Yes!" Nonnie cried out.

I didn't answer. The rats had halted, a squad in V-formation. Connoisseurs of choice morsels—of babies' satin cheeks, sucking thumbs, and tender colored buttocks—they neared the front for action.

"Come a little closer," I sneered.

"Oh, oh," Nonnie cried. "I can't wait to tell *him* about this moment! I am a *witness* of the principality!"

She was obviously nearly out of her mind, so I said only, "Patience, woman."

"Yes, my dear. But do hurry. He's beginning to kick. We're both excited."

I stood my ground. The rats seemed to be frozen in position, except for one glassy-eyed bastard, third from the end.

He broke ranks and came to meet me.

I flung my Dizzy Dean arms, made an effortless Jesse Owens leap, lunged like Johnny Unitas, and with my cleat-hard big toe kicked the rat clear across the room. He landed on Nonnie's caved-in sofa.

But I'll hand it to the others: they were brave little buggers, brilliantly poised for attack.

Strategy was extremely difficult. I had to map out a fast plan.

"Les, Les ... are you all right?"

"Yeah," I breathed and started to close up ground.

One rat, a second-stringer, made a leap but I crotched him with my right knee. He nose-dived, his skull going crack on the floor. Another zeroed in on that famed big toe, but I was ready for him too. Kicking wildly—because four were sneaking from the left flank—I could only knock him unconscious.

Now the four and I waltzed. One-two-left. One-two-right. One-two-left, one-two-right. One-two-left, one-two-rightonetwoleftonetwo—and then the biggest son of a bitch of all leaped as if he'd had airborne training.

I hunched down fast and he sailed right over my head. I spun around just in time to land a solid right in his sub-machinegun mouth.

Panting hard, I watched him go down slow, his head bobbing in a kind of ratty frug.

I felt good.

"They at war!" I heard Mrs. Tucker yell. I looked over at Nonnie. She was backed against the door, mesmerized with admiration.

When I turned to face the enemy again, two rats were retreating.

Pursuing as fast as I could, I slipped on the waxed floor and fell smack on the remaining three. But I fell easily and was careful not to damage the fur.

I lay there briefly, rolled over, and scouted for the deserters. Two were making a beeline for the wastebasket, which was brass and steel and filled with empty Fundador bottles.

I was decent. I waited until they thought they were safe, only to discover that they were actually ice-skating on the brandy bottles.

I knelt down and called, "Rasputin, Rasputin." They raised their exquisite heads and I put my hands in the wastebasket, grabbed both by the neck—I squeezed, squeezed until the fur around their neck flattened. It was easy.

"You can open your eyes, Nonnie," I said in a tired voice.

"A Good Man Is Hard to Find," the gal from Storyville sang.

I was tired. I made a V-for-victory sign, winked, and started skinning rats.

Someone knocked at the door.

Nonnie was excited. "Oh, Les. The welcoming commit-tee has formed already!"

"Wanna sub for me, cupcake."

"Delighted."

Another knock. "It's Mrs. Tucker, your next-door neigh-bor, and I couldn't help but hear what was going on …"

"There ain't no action in this joint, bitch," said Nonnie.

"I just wanted to offer my heartfelt congratulations to young Master Jefferson."

"Is that all you wanna offer him?" said Nonnie bitchily.

"Now that's no way to talk, Miss Swift, and you a Southern-bred lady."

"You're licking your old salty gums," Nonnie taunted. "You smell fresh blood. If you're hungry, go back to yo' plantation in Carolina."

"I will in due time, thank you." Mrs. Tucker withdrew in a huff.

"Go! Go!" Nonnie said, and turned abruptly and walked over to where I sat on the floor. "I guess you know those skins ain't tax-free," she said.

Engrossed in my job and thinking of The Deb, I did not answer.

"I could report you," Nonnie went on. "You don't have a license for rat killing."

"But *you* invited me over. You were afraid they'd kill you!"

"That's besides the point," Nonnie said sharply. "There are laws in this land that have to be obeyed."

"You didn't mention the law when you were trying to break down my door."

"Smart aleck! Ambitious little Romeo. I want a percentage on every perfect skin!"

"But I'm not gonna sell them," I said clearly.

"Listen, conkhead! You'll put nothing over on me."

"Never fear, cupcake."

"You try to outsmart me and I'll see your ass in jail if it's the last thing I do."

I looked up at Nonnie and laughed. Rat killing was a manly sport and there was always the warmth of good sportsmanship after the game. I split open the belly of Rasputin number nine. The rich blood gushed on the parquet and I thought of the long red streamers on a young girl's broad-brimmed summer hat.

"At least you could give me some for broth," Nonnie cried. "Don't be so mean and selfish. I'm only a poor widow and soon there'll be another mouth to feed."

I wasn't really listening to Nonnie; in my mind I saw the tawny face of The Deb, saw her rapture upon receiving the magnificent pelts. We would talk and laugh and later make love. My penis, which I have never measured, flipped snakewise to an honest Negro's estimate of seven-and-a-half inches.

THIRTEEN

Three hours later, I found myself with a slightly crushed Christian Dior box, jumping the sidewalk puddles, in which I saw the reflected solidity of Victorian brownstones. Despite the chilly drizzle, children seemed to be enjoying themselves on the fire escapes: laughing, singing, catching raindrops, telling dirty stories.

I walked along, blinking at the reflections in the pools, thinking of the children against the background of the harsh Harlem streets (but magical, all the same, stuffed with riches), and looking up now and then at the wet gray sky, only to be knocked out of my reveries by the sound of music.

It was blues, blues so real they'd make you hollow at five o'clock in the morning, no matter if you were alone or in the arms of your lover. These blues were coming out of a three-for-one bar and grill. I stopped for a moment and listened to Jimmie Witherspoon grind out "See-See Rider" on the jukebox. Through the steamy face of the grill, I saw hands working with the dexterity of an organ grinder, turning banquet-size slabs of barbecue spareribs on a spit. I could smell the spareribs, too. The crawlers in my stomach performed (Mr. Fishback's credit card carried no weight in three-for-one bar and grills), so I moved on down the street, past select pawnshops, fourth-hand boutiques, liquor stores. In a doorway, narrow as a telephone directory, I saw a group of young people sitting on the staircase, playing Charlie Mingus music. I didn't stop. Mingus always takes my energy away.

Nor did I stop a little farther on, hearing, from a storefront church, Gospel music. No, I didn't stop. I've been listening to Gospel music as far back as I can remember.

As I went on, I began to hear Spanish music. I was not far from Spanish Harlem, where no rose ever grows, but human and paper roses sometimes blossom in the street. The Deb's flat was here, in Harlem's International Zone.

She lived in a "real co-op," she had told me. The cooperation came from the police department; the commissioner had stationed bluecoats on split six-hour shifts at the entrance. Even so, a "society" murder had been committed in the entrance last Thanksgiving morning.

Walking up the flagstone path of the co-op, I recognized the Sunday afternoon bluecoat. He sported a frozen smile. Rumor said that a few of Harlem's more inventive citizens had (under the personal direction of Mr. Fishback) drained the blood from his body and that now 150-proof gin ran through his veins.

Offering a sunny, arctic smile, bluecoat eyed the Christian Dior box.

"Hi," I said, stepping smartly into the lobby. A hunk

of dung-colored plaster fell from the ceiling, which was frosted like a cake, missing my head by inches.

An old stoop-shouldered crone was standing opposite the mailboxes, stuffing beeswax into cracks of the wall.

"Excuse me," I said, "are you the concierge?"

The crone looked up. Her face was buttermilk yellow and granite hard. "The who?"

"The super."

"No. I am not the super and I ain't his wife. I just happen to live here."

"I'm sorry. Do you know if The Deb's in?"

The crone seemed interested. "Which one, Sonny?"

"The one on the ninth floor."

"Oh, her. She's in. But I don't know if she's busy or not …"

I clicked my heels, walked away, and bounded up the shaky staircase.

The strains of "Muslim Da-Da, Mu-Mu" (the Faust of rock 'n' roll) drifted from The Deb's pad, but nothing could blanket my schoolboy joy as I knocked on the solid door.

The doorknob fell off. Rolled, spun like a top. I watched until it stopped and then turned, certain The Deb would be spying through the peephole.

"Oh. It's you," were her first words when she opened the door. She wore a yellow robe. "Come on in *if* you gonna."

"Thanks," I said nervously.

"You almost missed me. I was just getting ready to go to Radio City Music Hall. In a taxi, so as not to miss the newsreel."

"I thought perhaps we'd go to some quiet bistro ..."

"You got any money?"

"Why must you *always* think of money?"

The Deb stared at me briefly. "You're a card," she said. "Did you know that?"

"Now, cupcake ... Look. Here is a little something I thought you might like." I held the box out.

"Oh. A present. What is it ... no, let me guess. The definite, collected rock 'n' roll records?"

"Guess again."

"It wouldn't be a blond Macy wig, would it?"

"Women," I sighed. The most fascinating, hypnotic— the strangest creatures on the face of the earth.

"Give it to," The Deb said and lunged at the box.

"Easy, baby," I said, brushing her hand aside. I tossed the Dior box casually on her rumpled bed and sat down on a sick chair that was vomiting straw.

The Deb's hands tore the box open. I yawned.

"Oh! Oh! Oh! Oh!"

Hot-eyed, I watched The Deb fling open her yellow robe and press the pelts against her naked body.

"Mr. Jefferson, you are *the* most thoughtful man!"

"Just a little token of my esteem."

The Deb switched over and gave me a wet smacking kiss on the forehead. It was a sugar-daddy kiss, but I was grateful to be in her alluring old-rose presence. Dimpled nipples brushed my chin; the scent of her body was fresh as dew. My hands prepared for travel.

"Now, Mr. Jefferson," The Deb warned.

"*Cup*cake ..."

"Men," The Deb sneered, breaking away. "You want the world but don't wanna pay the price. You don't know the first thing about gentleness, and I don't care what country you come from."

"Shut your trap," I commanded. A masterly manner just might work.

The Deb veered away from me and then stopped. "*What* did you say?"

"You heard me," I told her and stood up.

"If that's the way you feel," The Deb said, "I'll just play me a little music."

"Don't you touch that goddam machine!"

"It's mine," The Deb said, "and I meet the landlord coming up the stairs on the first day of each month."

"Don't give me that jazz," I said, and began to sulk.

"Your, your ... Wig looks very glamorous this afternoon,"

she said in a let's-make-up tone. "I really mean it. It's so dark and rainy out, it brings kind of a glow into the room."

"To hell with The Wig," I said, not really meaning it, but I was interesting in something more than sweet words.

"I love it. Really I do."

Without answering, but thinking clearly, I went up to the tawny smasher and gave a backhanded slap that threw her against the low bed.

"And I thought you came bearing gifts of love," she cried.

"But I did," I said, kneeling down and cradling her tear-stained face in my firm hands, thinking of that old cat Othello. But being only an average young man, living in a terrible age, cuffed by ambition, and now in love—I could only press her against me and hope.

"Les," she said softly.

It was a small triumph, a midget step past the gates of pain.

The Deb had an "important engagement" at eleven and I had to be up early for Monday-morning business, so I left promptly at 9 P.M. Just as I reached my own block, I saw white-uniformed men carrying a covered stretcher. The frame of the stretcher gleamed under the street light.

Nonnie and Miss Sandra Hanover were coming down the stoop. Miss Sandra Hanover was out of costume. She wore blue jeans and a man's raincoat.

"It's old Miz Tucker, Les. Poor old thing passed away about an hour ago."

"Yes," Nonnie said. "Thoughtless bitch. She had to kick off and me in the condition I'm in."

"That's too bad," I said.

"We're going to the funeral home and make arrangements," Miss Hanover said. "She's got no family, so we're shipping her back to her white folks in Carolina."

"Yes," Nonnie said vigorously. "That was her last wish. To have her remains sprinkled on the plantation's blue grass. She'll make excellent fertilizer, I'm sure."

"Where's Mr. Fishback?" I asked.

"Go up and look in your room," Nonnie said. "He stopped by after you so rudely walked out on me this afternoon. I saw you steal that fancy box off the garbage truck."

Fuming, I rushed up the stairs.

Two messages were stuck under my door. One was from Little Jimmie Wishbone and read:

URGENT. Must talk with you.
Please call me at this number.

But there was no telephone number on the matchbox cover. I picked up Mr. Fishback's note. It was written on Mr. Fishback's usual fancy paper, a pale gray, with a border of asphodels and black bleeding hearts. It read:

Lester Jefferson, this will come as a surprise STOP I
am leaving for the deep sea diver's club STOP On
Eleuthra Island which is in the Bahamas STOP From
there I will go by chartered plane to Toledo, Spain
STOP Will return in good time STOP

"—F——," I said. Hump Mr. Fishback. But what did he
mean: "Return in good time"?

FOURTEEN

The following morning was, naturally, Monday, warm, windless, with a calendar-blue sky. I was up at the crack of dawn. I shaved, took a bath, borrowed a cup of day-old coffee grounds from Nonnie Swift from which I brewed a fine pot of java. Sitting at the kitchen table over coffee and cigarettes (it pays to rise early: first one in the john, where I found a pack of unopened filter-tip cigarettes), I began reading a small leatherette-bound volume, *The New York Times Directory of Employment Agencies.* "Whatever the job, depend on a private employment agent to help you find it," it said. "You'll find more employment-agency jobs in *The New York Times*"—a statement I was extremely glad to hear, for I was in desperate need of a job.

Before the first cup of java had cooled, I started to read a listing of the employment agencies:

CAREER BLAZERS—

FLAME THROWERS *&* EXTINGUISHERS AGENCY

We Are Looking for Young Men On the Way Up!

We will find you any type of job that can be performed by a human being and not by computers. The fact that it sounds so ridiculous is what makes it so appealing and a step forward! Your very own human future! It wasn't too long ago that the idea of having humans in every major industry was thought to be a little "ridiculous." But now these dreams are realities. We must all look for new worlds to conquer. Being realistic at heart, we invite you to pay us a call at your convenience. Special service for those on lunch hour or for those waiting on the first major afternoon attraction at a 42nd Street cinema.

RESERVATION AGENCY is proud to announce that it has immediate openings for men and women who want to work as a member of a closely knit research institute, located in Huntsville, Alabama. This is an opportunity to provide support for the U.S. Defense program.

Activities involve analysis and evaluations of newly proposed weapons. In addition to a broad background, applicants must be thoroughly experienced or show some interest in the following: Discrimination, Simulation, Motivation, Meeting Head-on Aggressive Personalities.

To Arrange An Interview Kindly Call Our

New York Office

RESERVATION AGENCY

an equal opportunity employer

BOYS! GIRLS! Take your Pick! Come see us! We never charge! The men who will play an important part in your future pay! We know you are tired of ads that say start in

the mailroom or ads that say start selling homemade cook-
ies! Here is a partial listing of our weekly "specials":

GIRLS—No experience if you are alert and looking for a
dream future. But you must speak well, like to meet interesting people, and use telephone. Must be able to be ac-
commodating. After a rotating program of three intensive
weeks and, qualifying, you will be promoted fast—to men
and boys and sporting buyers. Don't be afraid. No real
speed. Our clients pay beginners $60, plus fast raises and
high bonuses.

BOYS—BOYS—BOYS wanted by large active Queens or-
ganization. Attractive. Boys who are interested and willing
to deliver and clean. Some weekend work. Routine. Boys
must be strong. Willing to work for giants. Vets preferred
but not required.

BOYS AND GIRLS! Procurement trainees. $55 as a
starter. Seeking specialists. Only high-pressure sales types
considered.

BOYS AND GIRLS UNLIMITED OPPORTUNITY AGENCY
ART PROMOTION EMPLOYMENT AGENCY
Position available as face retoucher. Requires skill in white
and black. Dyeing, bleaching, applying plastic. Light manu-
facturing. Mostly cold items in all areas. No pre-pack.
Frozen over 200 years. Please do not solicit. Our employ-

ees know of this ad. They have the incentive to succeed. Bacon is their specialty. Your salary is open.

MISS NATIONAL SECRETARY EMPLOYMENT AGENCY Famous company is seeking well-bred ladies to screen Ivy League grads. Terrific opty for real pro with understanding. No shorthand required but must be capable of setting up exhibits for out-of-town executives. If you are assigned to diversified secretarial duties—we pay your medical expenses in confidence. We enjoy our employees and are liberal with them. Good salary plus low-cost lunch.

EXPORT EMPLOYEE SEEKERS
The Opportunity of the Year!

If you could write your own ticket you'd probably leave out some of the things offered by our client. No children. Multi-million-dollar credit benefits. Tax-free and sugar white. Brains and fortitude—not required. Do you live in a slum area? Do you have the ability to sell? Fantastic response to our Negro sale. Acclaimed by top authorities.

If you think you qualify for this remarkable opportunity, please come to the East Side Air Terminal. Car necessary. Full transportation and monitoring. Paris. San Francisco. Hawaii. Take your pick. Our client asks us for men with vibrations. Men with a desire to succeed before 30! Men who are extremely active in extracurricular activities. Do you have the ability to reach top men and test, gas, debug, and interview? We are seeking safety maintenance men. Civil. Designing. No hand devices. This is a position entailing use of radar—malfunction performances as applied to manned space vehicles. No transients need apply. Our chief will be in New York. Liquidation is necessary.

ACT NOW!

When applying, please bring separation papers.

I closed *The New York Times Directory of Employment Agencies,* although there were still forty-six more pages of listings, lit a cigarette, and leaned back in my chair, thinking. You Are Not Defeated Until You Are Defeated, I thought. You must maintain a Healthy Outlook when seeking a job, I added.

So I threw the employment directory out of the window and made up my mind to see The King of Southern-Fried Chicken. I would become a chicken man. It wasn't work in the real sense of the word. The pay was $90 for five and a half days, plus all the chicken you could eat on your day off. Not many young men lasted long with the Fried Chicken King, but I'd stick it out until I could do better. At least, I consoled myself, the feathers were electrified.

For the truly ambitious, time truly flies. One hour later, I was crawling through the streets of Harlem on my hands and knees, wearing a snow-white, full-feathered chicken costume. The costume was very warm. The feathers were electrified to keep people from trying to pluck them out or kicking the wearer in the tail. So effective was the costume that I didn't even have to stop for traffic signals; traffic screeched to a halt for me. And, as I said, the pay was ninety per week. The Deb and I could have a ball! I planned to eat chicken only on my day off and that was free. I also figured that if I cackled hard and didn't quit, I was bound to get a raise. How many people are willing to crawl on their hands and knees, ten hours a day, five and a half days a week? For me that was not difficult: I was dreaming, not of a white Christmas, I was dreaming of becoming part of The Great Society. So I went through the March streets on my hands and knees and cried:

> *Cock-a-doodle-doo. Cock-a-doodle-do!*
> *Eat me. Eat now. All over town.*
> *Eat now at the* KING *of*
> *Southern-Fried Chicken!*

FIFTEEN

I did not let the first day get me down, although when I got home that night I could still hear the voices of pedestrians ringing in my ears.

"I bet he's tough."

"No, honey. He's a spring chicken if I ever saw one."

"Here chickie-chick!"

"Mama, can we take him home and put him on the roof so the dogs won't get to him?"

"He's white but I bet if you plucked those feathers off of him you'd find out he's black as coal."

"I bet he's the numbers man."

"No, baby. Probably pushing pot."

"You can't fool me. It's the police. I knew they'd crack down on all of these carryings-on. Just think. In broad daylight. On Times Square."

"Bill, he's just what we need for our next party."

"Wish I'd thought of that gimmick."

"I bet a quarter he's deaf and dumb. That ain't him talking. It's a machine inside of him."

"Think he can get us tickets for the ice-hockey game at the Garden?"

"I wouldn't be surprised. People in show biz have all kinds of connections."

"Why don't you ask him?"

"No. We'd have to slip him a fin or he'd be a smart aleck; that is, if the bastard can talk."

"I wonder if he's hot. Do you think he can see?"

"I think he's the one we saw on TV last night. Remember the one that was always clowning? 'You'll see me around town,' he said, and just when he was going to tell us where, that goddam commercial flashed on."

"Jesus! What some people won't do for money."

All in all, it had been a rather interesting day. Things were looking up. My ship was at last docking, and *I* was safely guiding her into port.

Feeling pretty good, around eight o'clock that night I joined the tenants of my building in the backyard. There a mandarin tree had taken root in a compost of garbage that we had been putting there for two years, trying to shame the landlord (we said) into a sense of responsibility.

It was like a holiday, a miracle in our backyard. I joined in the fun until I received a telephone call. Employed, a part of our national economy, I trotted into the building. Wait until Little Jimmie Wishbone hears about me, I thought happily.

But when I picked up the telephone I heard The Deb's voice: "I know what you are—you're a Nigger ..."

She laughed, but there was no connection between this laughter and the laughter I remembered.

"Those curls are the most beautiful thing I've ever seen,

and yes, I'm a business woman, but I sorta liked you. You always seemed to be walking a tightrope, smiling to beat the band 'cause you were happy. Talk about the numbers I meet! Baby, you really gave me a jolt. And you know what I'm gonna do now? I'm going out and get my short kinky head tore up. I'm gonna go out and get shot down. Stoned out of my ever-motherloving head. I'm gonna hit every bar and nightclub in Harlem. And I want you to stand there and *hold that receiver* until you hear the next word from me. Ha! That'll be the day ..."

I let the receiver drop from my hand, and started for my room. I'd planned to touch up my hair with Silky Smooth because the hood of the chicken costume had pressed my curls against my skull. But for the moment Silky Smooth had lost its groove.

As I was going up the stairs, stunned and unhappy, I met the perky party girl, Miss Sandra Hanover. A male-femme in sundown antelope costume and matching boots.

"Les," she cried. "I thought I'd have to leave without saying goodbye."

"Leaving?"

"Yes, love. Your mother is going to Europe with the call girl. She just married this millionaire. Just like in the movies, and I'm here to tell you! I'm going along as her personal maid. I'll ride the high seas in full regalia. Talk about impersonation!"

"That's great," I managed to say.

Miss Sandra Hanover gestured, like the great soignée Baker from St. Louis, MO. "Ain't it? I may even go into show biz in Europe. The truly smart-smart flicks always sport a dark face these days."

Ordinarily, the word "impersonation" would have interested me, would set me to thinking. But the only thought it brought me now was that my own impersonation had caused the death of a bright dream.

Finally, I managed to say, "That's great, doll. When you leaving?"

"Wednesday. At the stroke of midnight."

"Well. I'll see you later. I've gotta go to Madam X's."

"Madam X!" Miss Sandra Hanover exclaimed. "You must be off your rocker!"

"No," I said. "I'm not off my rocker. I wanna survive."

Madam X's is located in Harlem's high-rent district, in a real town house fronting the barrier of Morningside Heights and St. Nicholas Avenue. It looked faintly sinister to my eyes, so I stopped and hesitated. Quiet as a bird watcher, I read the neat hand-painted black-and-gold sign:

WANT TO KICK THE LOVE HABIT?
Madam X guarantees
that you will never fall in love again.
Low down-payment.
Easy terms can be arranged.
Open as long as there is love in this world.

Bleeding emotionally from The Deb's bullets, I wiped one long, slow tear from my left cheek, and I'm not a weeper. But something like dry ice had coated my heart. Was I brave enough to blot her out of my mind and life? Before I might decide I was not, I bounded up the stoop, went in through the marble arch (there was no door), and found myself in Madam X's presence. And it was as if we had known each other all our lives, as if we were mother and son.

Madam X was a very dark woman of undefinable age with a gentle clown's mask of a face. She wore a black, hooded cape that reached the floor, yet it did not seem to catch lint or dust. She proposed tea and I accepted.

"One or two lumps?" said Madam X.

"One lump, please."

"Lemon?"

"No, thank you. Lemon seems so artificial."

"That's what I've always said. I'm a very Oriental tea drinker. Adding lemon to tea defiles it, you might say."

"That's a fact, Madam."

"I thought you looked like a well-bred young man who'd appreciate the better things. The true things of life."

"Thank you, Madam X. You are the first lady of the land."

"Thank you, son. Ah, you're a lad after my heart."

"Your teapot *is* something!"

"Isn't it though? Faïence, from the Mediterranean. I always say, nothing is too good for my tea. Sometimes I use a brass pot, even a plain earthenware pot. It depends on my mood, the situation, you know."

"Oh. Yes, indeed."

"The tea ceremony is practically a lost art in the Western world."

"I understand it's dying in Boston. No one really observes the ritual."

"Pity. But I understand the Russians are quite fond of tea. I imagine it's sort of a crude affair, though."

Gingerly, I took a sip of tea. "This is great. The absolute end. Real boss."

"I'm glad you like it," Madam X smiled. "Horrid, horrid world. Everyone clamoring for cocktails. I suppose they drink themselves to death because they know they're hell-bound."

She paused and said, "Do you feel it, son?"

I gulped tea and belched.

"Do you feel it, son?"

"It's a mother-grabber."

"You're much too kind."

"I wouldn't lie."

"I always try to brew the finest."

"What's the brand?" I asked.

"Brazilian marijuana," Madam X said grandly.

"It's too much, baby."

Laughing softly, Madam X said, "A lad after my own

heart. But I've made a recent discovery. The state of Virginia, famed as it is for its tobacco, also grows the most wonderful marijuana. But please don't breathe it to a soul."

"On my word of honor."

"I understand Mr. Fishback is sponsoring you."

"Yes, and he's something else, too. He's in Europe now. Spain."

"Mr. Fishback is a very important man. But I don't quite cotton to his taste for deceased females. I might add, however, that we all have our own taste."

"That's true. I once collected stamps."

Madam X laughed merrily. "The things we think we want to be! I wanted to be the mad bomber, and then a city planner and an architect, so I could redesign Manhattan and make it beautiful and efficient. But that was before I became a saint."

"Manhattan is going to the dogs," I said. "I'm gonna move to Jersey."

Ignoring this statement, Madam X said, "Would you like another cup of tea, Lester?"

"In a moment, thank you."

"Yes," Madam X said. "The only way to appreciate marijuana is to brew it. Serve it hot and inhale the fumes, a custom in my family for many years." Pausing and smiling a stoned smile, she said, "Your bill has been taken care of. Mr. Fishback. You're very fortunate."

Fortunate? Suddenly I remembered The Deb. Forgetting myself, I shouted, "Fortunate, my ass! I'm in love and it's driving me crazy."

"Your troubles are over," Madam X said, proper and poised and very gentry (there was even something bouncy and braying about her voice). "I have *never* failed. I *could* be the most famous woman who ever lived. I prefer *not* to be selfish. Human emotions are my one and only charity. If there wasn't love in this country, just think what would happen to the economy! Now Negroes are dirt poor. They haven't got time to worry about love. After they've received their papers, their Nationalization papers, then it will be time enough for them to think about love. Personally, I think love is ridiculous. A *bourgeois* sin. Something that the devil invented to make mankind *nervous*. The only passion that's worth suffering for is a passion for hard, cold cash."

Gripping my teacup, I leaned forward. Was I hearing right? Was my high wearing off?

"Madam, Madam ..."

"Yes, Lester?"

"I, I, I ..."

"Do I shock you?" Madam X asked sweetly. "You have such beautiful hair."

"Do you really think so?"

"I do indeed. It's a pity that you will have to get rid of it."

"What do you mean?" I asked. I was unexpectedly

angry. I would have taken a swing at the old bat, except that she was a friend of Mr. Fishback's.

"Now, don't raise your voice at me. I am not hard of hearing. In fact, I hear everything. And you just do as I say."

Trembling, I managed to set my teacup down. "That ain't got nothing to do with love. My Wig, I mean, my Wig has nothing to do with it."

"Oh, but it does, lad," Madam X continued in the same sweet voice. "*All* vanity is fear. I bet you can't imagine that I once had hair as lovely as your Wig? Tresses worth a king's ransom, but there're precious few kings these days. Only humble saints, like myself, and Mr. Fishback."

"Your hair was never as beautiful as my Wig," I said boldly. "I don't care what color it was."

Madam X stiffened. She had the look of a Biblical figure. Crossing woodsy hands against her bosom, she smiled. The terrifying, disconcerting eyes were closed: Madam X had the innocent smile of a seven-year-old girl.

"You are the road to self-destruction," she chanted. "All is not lost, though. You may find the way, *despite* The Wig!"

I was really angry now. It was taking all my family training and self-control to remain calm.

"Don't try to put the bad mouth on me, old woman!"

"Never," Madam X intoned. She stood straight and tall. Then, with a great birdlike swoop, she sank to the floor.

Her head was bowed as if in prayer. The hood of her

cape slid off, and her perfectly shaped bald head revealed one magnificent twelve-inch-long whorl of *golden* hair. It made me shiver.

"I'll see you later, Madam," I said.

"No, you won't see me," Madam X warned, without looking up. "You'll see the *portrait* of Lester Jefferson, and he'll be *without* The Wig."

3

"... AND ONE FINE MORNING."

—SCOTT FITZGERALD

SIXTEEN

It was now morning all over America. It was also morning in Harlem. The first of April in the year of my National Life Derby, there was a doubtful sky, laced with soft white clouds. And although it was not the day of reckoning, my Dutch-almond eyes were open at 7:30 A.M., E.S.T.

My, how the chicken days were flying! Three weeks of crawling around town on my hands and knees had made me a minor celebrity. Still, I didn't like some of the things the people said about me. My true i-dent was a guarded secret. I refused to appear on television (I was afraid The Deb might be watching). I was hopeful of a reconciliation, although, according to the gossip columns, she had become Café Society's darling. When she had gone out to get her "head tore up," she had evidently done it in the best places, I reflected sourly.

Harlem's new beauty is the girl with the short natural hair. She has fabulous style; she has never needed beads and bangles like some Cleopatra types, and she never will.

—Dorothy Kilgallen

Short-haired smasher making Broadway scene is The Deb.
A swinging African princess incognito. —Walter Winchell

Everyone wants The Chicken cackling about town but he
belongs to The King of Southern-Fried Chicken. Last
night a well-known television star was heard saying: He
must be a fallen angel. He seems so lonely.
                                                    —Dorothy Kilgallen

Gothamville's latest cackle and delight is from The Southern-Fried Chicken.   —Walter Winchell

All that stuff in the papers and no one knew who I was.
Impersonating a chicken, cackling, I was alone. I'd go on
living by myself in my small airless room. I'd continue to
be a trapped person, and if I ever got to heaven, I'd ask
God one question: "Why?"

Meanwhile, I'd extol the delights of Southern-fried
chicken. But not today; today, thank God, was my day off.
I got out of bed and went slowly to the hall bathroom to
prepare for a fiesta, a ball, a non-feathered swinging day.

Lord, Lord! Should I get down on my knees and pray,
or kill myself? Was it a miraculous dividend, or another
smart son-of-a-bitching trick of the white people, or
Madam X or Mr. Fishback or Nonnie Swift and her Creole
magic? All I'd done last night was touch up The Wig with
a tablespoon of Silky Smooth and a teacup of lukewarm

water. Then I'd masturbated and gone promptly to sleep. And the sons-a-bitching chemicals in the pomade had cooked, baked. The Wig gleamed, a burnished red gold, more fabulous than ever.

At least I was the first. But soon there'd be millions of red-headed Negroes. I'd start a new chapter in American Negro history.

Would *Time* magazine review this phenomenon under Medicine, Milestones, The Nation, Art, Show Business, or U.S. Business? Would the children of red-headed Silky Smooth parents have red- or kinky- or mixed-colored hair? Mixed, maybe, like a Yorkshire terrier? Would there be a new type of American Negro? Red-headed American Negroes, a minority within a minority? An off-color elite? And would that be a good thing? Maybe not. There'd be some Negroes (and *other* racially sick people) who'd be ready to beat the living hell out of red-headed Negroes just because they were not like other Negroes. One couldn't accuse red-headed Negroes of going white, or could one? Would white people hate or love red-headed Negroes more than they loved or hated other Negroes? Would white people find red-headed Negroes sexually attractive?

All these questions were pouring in on me. "Mother of God," I cried helplessly, gripping the edge of the wash-basin with all my strength. No good. I made a mad leap over to the john just in time.

As the tensions left my naked body, exhaustion set in. I

was in no condition to deal with the possible problems of my Wig. I listlessly heard the sweet cries of children in the hall, pleading not to be sent to school (an imposing red-brick structure that had split in half for some strange reason the week before, killing twenty children, all under the age of twelve). Nonnie Swift had cackled happily about it ever since. Her son, she said, would be tutored at home.

A New York mockingbird chirped in the mandarin tree.

I went back to my room but I couldn't stay there. I had to get out. Out and walk, walk and try not to think. I wanted to scream to anyone, to the sky: "But I didn't mean anything! All I wanted was to be happy. I didn't know to want to be happy was a crime, a *sin*. I thought sin was something you bought for ten dollars a major ounce and five dollars a minor ounce, both qualities highly recommended, and each wrapped in plain brown paper. I never bought any—not because I couldn't afford it. I just took pot for a dollar a stick …"

But why go on? Why try to explain? Was there anyone to hear me?

I dressed hurriedly and, magnificently Bewigged, went out, locked the door, and walked slowly down the steps, thankful that Nonnie Swift was not about.

Half of a neatly folded telegram stuck out of my mailbox. Filled with apprehension, I ripped the telegram open. It read:

I bet you can't guess where I am at. I wasn't doing nothing. These colored clubwomen wanted me for a benefit but the white clubwomen said I wasn't college. At least not Ivy and queer. The colored clubwomen agreed. I wished you could have heard the names they called me after the white clubwomen had left. I wasn't doing nothing but walking through the streets looking for my lavender Cadillac number three and the bluecoats arrested me for nothing at all. I only had a quart of Summertime wine and was just drinking. I paid for it, didn't I? So why can't I drink it on the street? So I'm back here. The white devils. I was getting ready to do a profile on TV, too, with Mr. Sunflower Ashley-Smithe. Don't worry none, though. They got a cell ready for you. Next to mine. How long you think the white devils gonna let you go through the streets with your hair looking like that? Why didn't you phone me? I left my number.

Little Mr. Jimmie Wishbone

Despite the springlike air, goose pimples peppered my body. The nut ward at Kings County! Lord—and all I'd wanted was to breathe easier.

I tore up the telegram, threw it into the air like confetti. The sky was clear and blue. A glazed sun highlighted the Harlem skyline. Looking at that skyline, I remembered what Mr. Fishback had once said to me. "Lester Jefferson,"

Mr. Fishback had said—it was on my sixteenth birthday—
"you're almost a man. It's time you learned something.
That Harlem skyline is the outline of your life. There is
very little to discover by looking at the pavement."

I didn't know what he meant then, and I didn't know
now. If I asked him—and I had asked—he'd just say,
"You're on your own for now. *My presence won't be required
until ... "*

As if I wasn't aware that he was always, always around,
hovering over me. He was a prime mover of people, a
black magician. But it was the first of April, and too many
things had happened, and Mr. Fishback was in Spain, or
somewhere. Perhaps I didn't need him as yet.

I walked over to Lenox and 125th Street, where I joined
a group of Black Muslims standing in front of the Theresa
Hotel. The Muslims had flutes and flowers and were making joyous sounds. They were hawking chances on a spe-
cially built armored tank that was guaranteed to go from
New York City to Georgia and back on one gallon of gas.
The chances were only twenty-five cents.

"I ain't never going back to Georgia," one man exclaimed. "Why don't you have something that will take me
to Biarritz or Cuernavaca? That's more like my speed."

Gradually, the crowd grew bored and drifted away. I
moved on down the avenue to where a sneaker-shod
young man, pink-jacketed with pink low boy trousers,

sold French poodles. "Be like the fashionable common masses," he shrilled in a vaguely cultured voice. "Own a real French poodle sired by Chee of New Jersey and Dame Chowder of Staten Island. Poodles are the latest rage. Everyone has a smart French poodle. Why not you? Poodles should be clipped twice a week. You can use the left-over curls for your own head. The latest word in African hair styles. And these genuine French poodles are only thirty-nine dollars and ninety-nine cents, plus neighborhood, city, county, state, and federal sales tax."

But I needed no poodle curls; I was my own Samson, a Samson with Silky Smooth hair. My true glory had flowered, I thought bitterly, remembering Nonnie Swift's words.

"Poodles, poodles," the sneaker-shod young man called after me, but I crossed the street and went on my way.

"Look at him," a small boy cried, pointing his bony hand at me. "I bet *he* ain't going to school!"

Smiling, I said, "No, Sonny. Not today."

"But *he's* going to school," the boy's mother said to me, doubling a suede-gloved fist and slamming it against the boy's mouth.

"Jesus, he must be a very bad boy," I said.

"He is," the mother said vigorously.

I stared hard at the crying boy. "What did he do?"

"He doesn't want to go to a segregated school. I broke my broom handle on him a few minutes ago. That's what the NAACP and the Mayor and the Holy Peace-Making Brotherhood advised. You wouldn't have a pistol on you, would you?"

"No," I shuddered. A sudden pain hit me so hard that I felt faint.

My throat was dry. "Isn't there some other way you can make the boy understand?"

"No," the mother replied.

"Maaa," the boy moaned. "Please take me to the hospital. I ache all over. I think I'm gonna die, Mama."

"Shut your trap."

Just then a soothsayer wearing a dark policeman's uniform walked up twirling his nightstick.

"What's wrong, lady? Having trouble with your boys?"

"Only the little one," the mother laughed. "He doesn't want to go to a segregated school. I've got to beat some sense into the boy's head if it's last thing I do."

"Wanna use my nightstick? I'm sorry I don't have my electric cow-prod with me because that does the trick every time. That always makes them fall in line."

"Oh, officer," the mother said, "you're so kind and understanding."

"Think nothing of it. Just doing my duty. I've got kids of my own. I certainly wouldn't want them to go to an integrated school."

"Now, wait a minute," I said angrily. "This isn't fair!"

"Buster," the policeman said, "do you want me to knock

that grease out of your hair? I'll get you thirty days in the workhouse. You're trying to obstruct justice."

Silently, I watched the mother slam the nightstick against the boy's head. The boy's mouth opened and he fell to the sidewalk. Blood flowed from his nostrils and lips. "Mama," he sighed, and closed his eyes.

"Get up from there, you nasty little thing," the mother cried. "Get up. Do you hear me? Just look at you, and I stayed up half the night getting your clothes clean and white for school."

"I think the boy's dead," I said.

"He ain't dead," the policeman said. "He's just pretending because he doesn't want to go to school."

The mother knelt down and shook the boy and then stood up. "He's dead," she commented in a clear voice. "I could never talk to him."

"It's not your fault," the policeman said. "Kids are getting out of hand these days."

I tottered off, knowing that I couldn't eat any free fried chicken even if it was my day. I hadn't been to a church in a very long time and I thought I might go to one, but then I remembered that all of the churches in Harlem were closed. The Minister's Union had declared April first to be a day of soul-searching, a day devoted to making money, a day of solitude for the ministers whose nerves had failed them.

So I veered on to Eighth Avenue and 116th Street,

where all was quiet except for a rumble on the west side of the Avenue. Fourteen shoeshine boys were fighting savagely with a gleaming six-foot Negro man. The shoeshine boys were winning.

One ferocious shiner jumped me. "Are you a shiner?" he asked.

"Not today," I said.

"Where is it at?" the six-foot man asked. "I'll call the police on you little black bastards."

"Call'm," the shoeshine boys chorused. "We ain't done nothing against Lily Law."

"That's right," the ferocious shiner said. "We ain't done nothing. We just invented this dust machine to help our business downtown. The dust shoeshine boy stands on the corner with the machine in a shopping bag from Macy's, rolling his white eyeballs and sucking a slice of candied watermelon. You know. Like he's waiting on his mama. Every time a likely customer walks by, the dust shiner pulls the magic string. By the time the customer reaches the middle of the block he sure need a shine. He our gravy. And now this mother-grabber is gonna call Lily Law. He wants to suck white ass. He ain't thinking 'bout us little black boys."

The gleaming tall man broke away and ran inside a diner. "I'll fix you little devils."

"I'll go inside and see what I can do," I told the shoeshine boys. "Now you boys run like crazy."

I wasn't a hero and I've never aspired to be one (except in a private, loverly sense—ah, The Deb), but I've always, always, tried to help people. It's a kind of perverse hobby with me. Opening the diner door, I offered a diplomatic grin. The gleaming man was on the telephone.

"Mr. Police. This is Jackson Sam Nothingham. Yes sir. The Black Disaster Diner. What do you mean … It's me, Mr. Police. Your sunny-side-up boy. That's right."

The diner owner hadn't noticed me. I eased over and deftly pulled the phone cord from the wall.

"What? I can't hear you. Say something, Mr. Police. I pays my dues … And what's more, I takes care of the Captain when he comes around …"

"Maybe they hung up on you, Mac," I said.

The bewildered owner swung around. "What you mean, boy? They hung up on me? Wait until the Captain gets a load of this. He knows I sell a little gin and whiskey in coffee cups after hours. All the Mister Polices on this beat says they don't know what they'd do without good old Jackson Sam Nothingham. My good down-home Southern cooking and a nip on a cold rainy day. I'm keeping up the morale of the police force and you try to say they hung up on me?"

"That's the way the cookie crumbles," I philosophized. "It doesn't have to be a Chinese fortune cookie either."

The angry tall man looked hard at The Wig. "You curly-headed son-of-a-bitch. Git out of here. Git out of the Black

Disaster Diner. I am the owner and I refuse to serve you. All you spicks and niggers are the cause of my troubles."

"If that's the way you feel about it," I said.

"Git out," the tall man shouted. His whole body trembled. "You people are ruining me. I've been in business twenty years and the white people have loved me and I've been happy."

He slumped down into a cane-backed chair like a wounded animal.

If that is how he feels, there's nothing for me to say, I thought, and, lowering my eyes, I walked briskly out of the Black Disaster Diner.

Now the sun was behind the clouds; there was the quiet of mid-morning except for the sound of singing, coming from an open window.

Singing was another world as far as I was concerned, although I was capable of producing a rooster's resonant crow. And it felt a little strange to be walking like a human being on the first of April. Strutting around Manhattan on my hands and feet was good exercise, I'd discovered.

By the time I reached Central Park and Ninety-sixth Street, four Puerto Ricans stopped me.

"*Español?*"

"No," I laughed, trying to break a gut string. I understood. It was The Wig. I realized that many Puerto Ricans wanted to lose their identity. Many of them pretended to be Brazilians. It was not only safer, it was chic. Puerto Ricans had inherited the dog trough vacated by the Negroes.

Burnished-red-golden-haired Puerto Ricans were extremely rare, as were burnished-red-golden-haired Negroes, I sadly reflected, crossing at Seventy-second Street and Central Park.

I walked along, magnificently Bewigged, shoulders erect, firm hands jammed in my blue jeans, jingling nickels and pennies, calm and a little lonely.

Suddenly I wanted to talk to someone; hoped someone would say, "Good morning. What lovely weather we're having." "Yes. Isn't it?" I'd reply. "I think we'll have an early spring." "I hope so," the other party would say. "Of course, you never can tell." "That's right," I'd say. Corny human stuff like that.

I was rehearsing the imaginary dialogue when I smiled at a middle-aged woman with a face that looked as if it had stared too long at the walls of too many furnished rooms. The middle-aged woman's tiny pink eyes went from my smiling face to The Wig. She leaned back on the bench, opened her mouth, and shut her eyes tight.

Well, I thought, moving on, she is not accustomed to beauty.

An elderly couple were eying me. I heard the man mutter to his wife: "It's all right, Wilma. Times are changing. Remember the first automobile? World War One? We can't

escape what we've never dreamed because we've always
believed it was impossible. Wilma? Please don't cry. We'll
be dying soon. *And then we won't have to look at such sights."*

He meant me.

The sight went calmly on, smiling at a fat Negro who
carried a shopping bag with Silky Smooth printed on the
side. The fat Negro woman spat tobacco juice at my shoes,
and a blond Alice-in-Wonderland type urinated in a plastic
sand bucket and tried to splash me. Her mother applauded.

I was beginning to get a little sore. I felt like saying,
"Nothing, nothing—do you hear me—nothing can stop
me." Who the hell did they take me for? Was I the young
man who had ground three hundred pounds of chopped
meat out of the bodies of seventy blind people? Or the
young man who had rescued a pregnant mother and her
five children from their burning home, and then single-
handed built them a ranch house overnight? Was I the
champion rod who had respectively screwed wife, husband, mother-in-law, part-time maid, twelve-year-old
daughter, fourteen-year-old son, white parrot, and family
collie pup?

No! I was the celebrated chicken man, and none of
them knew it. Ten hours a day, five and a half days a week,
crawling on my hands and knees all over Manhattan. And
I'd been a target for such a long time. Five-foot-ten, naked
without shoes, normal weight 140 pounds. Boyish, with a

rolling non-nautical gait, my face typically mixed: chamber-pot-simmered American, the result of at least five different pure races copulating in two's and three's like a game of musical chairs.

Following my own shadow, it seemed that I was taking a step in *some* direction and that The Wig was my guide. Progress is our most important product, General Electric says, and I had progressed to the front door of hell when all I had actually been striving for was a quiet purgatory. And I did not find it strange that hell had a soft blue sky, a springlike air, music, dust, laughter, curses.

I only wished I could see a friendly face.

Up ahead I saw a girl wearing what seemed to be a white mink coat. I checked my stride. A trick of nature or a goddam trick of my eyes? I neared the girl. My blood began to percolate. She was different. Blue-black shiny hair. Complexion: light brown, or did it have an Oriental cast, or was it a trick of the light? The girl's dark eyes were heavily lidded. The lips might have belonged to a beautiful woman of any race. But what was her actual nationality? Mulatto? American Indian? East Indian? Italian?—she had a mustache of moisture on her upper lip and I had been schooled in the folklore of Italian women by printed matter. There was a hint of warmth in her marvelous dark eyes; so it was extremely possible that she was a beauty from North Africa. She might even be Jewish, I thought, remembering that beautiful Jewish girl on West Eighty-seventh Street.

I would die if the girl was simply a dark Gentile.

I was about ten paces from her, when the sun blazed forth. Traffic around the circle was jammed.

The girl said, "I've been waiting for you."

"And I've been waiting too," I found myself saying.

"I've been waiting for someone exactly like you."

"You're beautiful. You don't have to wait for anyone."

The girl smiled warmly. "No. You're wrong," she said. "Are you coming with me?"

I nodded doubtfully but I took the girl's arm. "All right. I'm game. Where are we going?"

"Just keep in step with me. I've been so lonely," she said, "I feel like I'm living in the desert, though actually I'm living in a great city with millions of people."

"I've often felt like a hermit, too," I said. Was this chick stoned? She didn't look it.

"I know. I know. Now it'll be different for us. I've got a lifetime of love to give and I couldn't give it to just anyone. Understand?"

"Yeah," I replied, beginning to relax. Man, The Wig was really working! "I know what you mean."

"Most people are not very nice, are they?"

"No. Most people are not very nice."

Then we were silent. We danced arm in arm across Central Park West and up the five steps of a very respectable brownstone, just as the siren, like a proclamation, announced twelve o'clock.

The girl's two-rooms-and-kitchenette were very clean. There were no cockroaches, rats, mice, no leeches, no tigers.

Softly feminine, the girl said, "Relax, baby."

Then she came over and tried to rip the button-down shirt from my body.

"Take it easy, baby," I said, biting her neck. "We have all the time in the world."

"I know, I know," she said contritely, "but I must have this release."

She elbowed me so hard that I fell backward on to a big brass bed, where she proceeded to remove my loafers, socks, and blue jeans. I wore no shorts because the chicken costume was very warm.

The girl kissed the soles of my feet.

"Come on up here," I said, feeling my kingly juices.

"You have beautiful strong legs."

I kicked her lightly on the chin, she fell back on the floor. I jumped off the bed. Ready, at attention. She whimpered. I mounted her right on the floor. She sighed and patted my forehead. I sighed. Irritable, I also frowned. "Let's cut the James Bond bit. Let's get this show on the road."

The girl sank her teeth into my right shoulder. I slapped her hard and carried her to the bed. She whimpered again. I fell on top of her. Her tongue was busy in my left ear. I whimpered. Her right hand, like a measuring tape, grabbed my penis.

With my right hand I cupped her chin and thrust my tongue into her throat.

The girl squirmed and tickled my ribs.

Lowering her head, I kissed her chin and the oyster opening of her neck where her bone structure V'd, until my face slid farther down, and came to rest in the soft luxury of her breast. More delicious than fruit, I thought, teasing the wishbone below her breasts.

Still going down, I stopped at her navel.

She said clearly, "Oh," and rose slowly.

Panting, I shoved her back down on the bed, and with my knees, opened her legs. They opened like a pretty, well-constructed fan, and then closed like a fan, engulfing my back.

"Mercy," I sighed, settling in.

She bit my lower lip but didn't say anything. I did not say anything either. But at the climax, I bit *her* lower lip. Her hands were mad on my back.

Now I was breathing deeply; my eyes kept closing. The girl sighed. Then her sharp teeth nipped my cheek with its day-old beard. Pleased, she went on to discover the delight of my nose, the treasure of my ears, my red but large eyeballs. And then, like one looking for truffles, she buried her face against my flat hairless chest.

"Baby," I whispered.

"Love," she said.

I looked tenderly into her smiling face, planted one sounding kiss on her nose. Then I fell against her, and the last thought I had before dozing off to sleep was, "I wonder what The Deb is doing?"

I was awakened by having my neck kissed.

"I've got love to give," the girl said, digging her fingernails into my backsides.

"Sweetcakes," I sighed, coming to life again.

"I just want to make you happy."

"And I want to make you happy," I said.

"Do you love me a little?"

I was feeling much too good to answer.

The first shadows of evening arrived. There was no moon, I noted through the sheer white curtains. And there were no stars. In the room, there was only the glow of the girl's shining hair and the glow of The Wig.

Silently, she anointed my body with joy.

Yawning, I said, "I wanna Coke, and put some ice in it."

"Yes, love," she said.

Smiling in the darkness, I put my hands behind my

head. I felt good. The frustrations of the day had been spent. The Wig, The Deb, and all those people I had encountered …

"Love," the girl called, breaking into my thoughts.

She sat down on the side of the bed and took me in her arms and held the glass of iced Coke as she would for an ill child. With her free hand, she gently stroked my brow.

"I want you to become my lover," she said quietly.

"We've just met," I protested. "We don't even know each other."

"You'll learn to love me. I'm a good woman. I've got money."

I bolted up from the bed. "Where's my jeans? I gotta run, cupcake. Perhaps I'll see you later."

"Please," the girl cried.

"Later," I said softly. I got into my clothes and made it to the door. Just as I shut it behind me, I thought I heard her cry, "I'm going to tell Mr. Fishback on you!"

Midnight found me on the Eighth Avenue A train for Harlem, wearing a pretty flower-printed plastic rainhood I'd luckily snatched up along with my clothes. It was raining out, and otherwise I'd have got The Wig wet. None of the passengers paid me the slightest attention. They had witnessed too many extraordinary happenings on subway trains: such as an old man getting stomped to death by a group of young punks because he didn't have life insurance; or someone getting sick and choking to death. Even statutory rapes had lost their appeal, they'd seen too many of them—so no one was likely to be impressed by a sad-faced, red-eyed young man wearing a plastic rainhood, shivering, biting his fingernails, staring at his reflection in the dirty window of the car.

I began to doze, thinking: when love waxes cold, said Paul in "The Third Coming ..." then jerked up suddenly as the A train pulled into 125th Street.

I was the only passenger to get off. The platform was deserted. Workmen were spraying the platform with glue. Dazed and a little frightened, I ran up the sticky steps and out into the deserted street and hailed a taxi.

The driver, wearing a gas mask, stuck his head out the window.

"Oh, it's you," said Mr. Fishback, the funeral director. He removed the gas mask, spat false teeth on to the sidewalk. Then he placed a fresh pair of false teeth in his mouth. "It's this goddam country. It's ruining my health. I can't complain, though. They're dying every second. But there won't be anybody around to beautify me when I kick off. Ain't that a bitch?"

I had a sudden urge to rip the taxi door off. "Why are you driving a Yellow Cab?"

"I was waiting for you, Lester Jefferson," Mr. Fishback

said innocently. "Why, they brought this big fat mama in and I didn't even have a chance to bang her. Terrible to see them go into the ground before you get what you want. And I didn't wanna upset you by arriving in my hearse."

"Why should that upset me? I've been riding in your hearse all my life."

For reasons known only to him, Mr. Fishback replaced the gas mask. "When love waxes cold ..."

"What?" I exclaimed. "You been experimenting again?"

"The Deb," Mr. Fishback began. "She got run over by a school bus this afternoon."

Numbed, I could only stare at Mr. Fishback. I took off the rainhood.

"No," Mr. Fishback said solemnly. "You know she had been taken up by café society and was staying high all the time. You had made her see things she had never seen before. Madam X said she called for an appointment but never showed. Under that tough, tart front, she was a sweet kid. An all-American girl. She left her rock 'n' roll record collection to charity. But I might be able to get you a couple of favorites."

"Mr. Fishback," I said, "it's strange, The Deb is dead but *my* heart's still beating, and I can't cry."

"It happens in all the best families and to the world's greatest lovers."

"Yes, that's true."

"Get in, son," Mr. Fishback said kindly. "Rest assured, The Deb is in the best of hands."

"I know," I said, "but I won't get in, thank you."

"She's a beautiful dead girl."

"Yes. Now please drive slow. I'll walk along beside you. That's the least I can do for her."

"Do you need my gas mask?"

"No."

"It's dangerous."

"I don't care," I said.

Mr. Fishback's mortuary was under the Triboro Bridge, at the edge of the polluted, muddy river. It was a one-story building of solid plate glass, with the roof also of glass, rising up dramatically like the wings of a butterfly. Mr. Fishback parked the taxi (which belonged to his brother-in-law, who was dying, he said), near the bridge and then walked down a lonely garbage-littered slope with me.

Side by side, we walked under a deep gray sky that was just beginning to break with the first light of day. The cool air was refreshing against my feverish face.

Once, for a brief moment, I panicked. "I can't go on."

"Now, son," Mr. Fishback said gently.

"What can I do now?"

"You know what you have to do."

"Yes," I nodded, clutching Mr. Fishback's arm for support.

We entered the glass building and walked like mourners to the direct center of the floor. Marble tiles slid back. Mr. Fishback removed his mask. He had a kind, dark, wrinkled face, the face of a genius, though being modest, he had always considered himself just God.

He escorted me down steps into a room the size of a standard bathroom. The room was mirrored and brightly lit, odorless. There was only a red bat-wing chair.

"I'm glad to get rid of these things," Mr. Fishback said, jerking out his false teeth and spitting blood on the floor. "Everything is so unsanitary!"

I flopped into the bat-wing chair: "The poor Deb!"

"Hush, now. You'll feel better after I cut off The Wig. Then one more act and you'll be happy for the rest of your life. While I was abroad, I kept in touch with Madam X. Remarkable woman."

Mr. Fishback pressed an invisible button in the mirrored wall and out popped a brand-new pair of sheep shears.

I closed my eyes. I felt no emotion. It was over. Everything. Love waxed cold. The Deb—dead.

"Watch out for my ears," I warned. "And hurry up. I'm hungry."

There were tears in Mr. Fishback's eyes as he expertly clipped The Wig in exactly one minute.

"It was so beautiful," he sniffed.

I kicked the magnificent burnished red-golden hair

haloed around the wing chair. I smiled at my baldheaded reflection. "It's over. I can always do it again."

"It was so pretty," Mr. Fishback said. "Nobody had hair like that except Madam X, and that was before she became a saint."

"She's a funny woman. She gave me the creeps. I didn't stay for the first session."

"I know," Mr. Fishback said sharply. "Now stand up and take off your clothes."

"Why?"

"Just do as I say."

"You're always experimenting." I laughed weakly, but I stood up and stripped.

Mr. Fishback sighed. "You've lost weight. You look like a corpse. Think of something nasty and get an erection."

"Like what, for example?"

"Anything. Hell. This country is filled with nasty images."

"The Deb and I will never have children. Why are you torturing me!"

"Not so loud," Mr. Fishback said angrily. "Having children is the greatest sin in this country, according to Madam X. After a series of experiments, Madam X has concluded that having children is a *very* great sin. Hate is an evil disease."

"I've got an erection," I said.

"Fine," Mr. Fishback said happily. He pushed another invisible button in the mirrored wall and out popped a red-hot slender steel rod.

With a deadly-serious expression on his face, Mr. Fishback jabbed the steel rod into the head of my penis.

He counted to ten and jerked it out.

Sighing hard, he asked, "How do you feel?"

"I'm beginning to feel better already," I said, smiling.

CHARLES STEVENSON WRIGHT was born in New Franklin, Missouri, in 1932. At the age of eighteen he attended the James Jones & Lowney Turner Handy Writer's Colony in Marshall, Illinois. A former columnist for the *Village Voice* ("Wright's World"), he has also written for *Vogue* and *The New York Times*. He served two years in the U.S. army, the last year in Korea. He is the author of three published works: *The Messenger* (1963), *The Wig* (1966), and a "journal-novel" *Absolutely Nothing to Get Alarmed About* (1973). He lives in New York City.

ISHMAEL REED, a preeminent figure of contemporary African American letters, has been nominated twice for the National Book Award (for *Conjure* and *Mumbo Jumbo*). A lecturer at University of California, Berkeley, he lives in Oakland, where he runs Ishmael Reed Publishing, Co. (www.ishmaelreedpub.com).

THE MESSENGER

"A very beautiful job ... And, no matter what the city fathers may say, this is New York; this the way we live here now. Charles Wright is a terrific writer."

—JAMES BALDWIN

"Savage and vivid." —THE NEW YORK TIMES

"Haunted, human and real ... honest, tough—and compassionate." —HARPER'S

THE WIG

"Charles Wright's Negro world explodes with the crazy laughter of a man past caring.... His style, as mean and vicious a weapon as a rusty hacksaw, is the perfect vehicle for his zany pessimism.... *The Wig* is a brutal, exciting, and necessary book." —THE NEW YORK TIMES

"In this unrelenting satire Mr. Wright has taken even the most minor cliché (uttered by Black or White) and turned it inside out. Not contented with that, he has taken a few of the major ones and carried them to their logical—and absurd—conclusions. It is all done with a matter-of-fact bitterness which never allows the comic and the horrific to drift too far apart. And it rings sickeningly true."

—LONDON TIMES LITERARY SUPPLEMENT

ABSOLUTELY NOTHING TO GET ALARMED ABOUT

"Charles Wright has written with his own blood, in compassion, humor, and despair, a book about the human condition that takes its place among the most honest testimonials of our time."
—KAY BOYLE

"It would diminish Charles Wright to call him merely an important black writer. Such talent as his transcends race: his concern is with the entire human condition."
—ANTHONY BURGESS

"Charles Wright is the aristocratic poet-in-residence of America's seamy side. He doesn't flay so much as haunts."
—ISHMAEL REED

"Charles Wright is one of the best. He has worked out a language and a landscape that is a kaleidoscope of mystery and simplicity, filled with miracles and puzzles. His is an almost effortless style that works. There is humor and a kind of unholy wisdom.... When I say he's a good writer I don't say that lightly."
—CLARENCE MAJOR

THE NEA HERITAGE & PRESERVATION SERIES CELEBRATES
THE MULTICULTURAL DIVERSITY OF AMERICAN LETTERS WITH
MODERN CLASSICS OF CULTURAL IDENTITY.

ALSO IN THIS SERIES:

JOSÉ ANTONIO BURCIAGA
            IN FEW WORDS/EN POCAS PALABRAS
            A Compendium of Latino Folk Wit & Wisdom

SADAKICHI HARTMANN
            A SADAKICHI HARTMANN READER

WE THANK THE NATIONAL ENDOWMENT FOR THE ARTS
FOR THEIR CONTINUED SUPPORT.